IN THE
MAGICIAN'S HOUSE

Another 'You Say Which Way' Adventure
by
DM Potter

Published by:
The Fairytale Factory Ltd.
Wellington, New Zealand.

ISBN-13: 978-1522965961
ISBN-10: 1522965963

How This Book Works

- This story depends on YOU.

- YOU say which way the story goes.

- What will YOU do?

At the end of each chapter, you get to make a decision. Turn to the page that matches your choice – for example, **P62** means turn to page 62.

~~~

Dreams swirl around in the Magician's house like dust in the corners of other houses. Little stories get stuck in the crannies. Just for a moment, while you are sweeping, you can find yourself running across a green field, steering an iron horse through twisty roads, or picking ripe strawberries in a bright, warm field. Other times you are transported to different places, so you watch where you step. Some mornings, just getting to breakfast is an adventure.

In the Magician's House

In your turret

You can't remember a time before you lived in the Magician's house. There are many rooms, but finding them is not always easy. The house is cloaked in mystery, and you explore it every day.

You find the kitchen most mornings. You follow the lovely smells and don't think too hard about it. Perhaps your recent dreams help you get to breakfast without much trouble. More likely, it's because the Magician wants his breakfast.

You can find most places in the house, so you're often asked to fetch things. The other servants get lost more often than you do. Sometimes you find them in the corners of rooms and give them a friendly pat to bring them out of a 'drawing room dream'. That is what the cook, Mrs. Noogles, calls them.

Dreams swirl around in the Magician's house just like dust in the corners of other houses. Little stories get stuck in the crannies. Just for a moment, while you are sweeping a corner, you can find yourself running across a green field, speaking to a great crowd, steering an iron horse through twisty roads, or picking ripe strawberries in a bright warm field. The dreams are quickly over, but other times you are transported to different places. So you watch where you step.

It is very early in the morning, and you wake up in your turret. It is your own tower with a winding staircase down to the house.

Something lands on your pillow and rolls against your cheek, cold and small. You put your hand out. It's that red frog again. It stares at you, unblinking. You put it carefully with your other treasures and oddities.

The sky is dark purple, with one last star valiantly blinking as the sun turns your corner of the world into day. You love looking out of your tower window and catching the day starting like this — in this moment the whole world is magic, not just the place you live.

Down the spiral staircase, on the next floor, you wash the sleep from your eyes and put on fresh clothes. A noise like a marble falling down the stairs becomes the sound of a rubber ball until the red frog appears with a final splat. He takes a quick dip in the big jug of water you keep for him there. When he jumps out, he doesn't leave any wet marks on the flagstone floor. He seems to absorb moisture. The jug is now only half-full.

By the window, a row of ants are marching across the floor. The frog jumps over to the row of insects, and whips out his tongue to catch ant after ant until the column is gone. If only getting *your* breakfast was that easy.

Outside the window, you can see the buildings of London — St Paul's cathedral is a beautiful dome by the river Thames. Horses and carts make their deliveries down the twisty lanes. Much of London is still sleeping, but servants are stirring to light the fires and make their master's breakfast. You must tend to your master too.

You wonder which room your tower will join with today. Sometimes it will deliver you to a hallway that easily gets you to the servant's staircase and down to the kitchen, but often there is another destination at the foot of the stairs. Things are seldom as they appear. You have learned to be cautious in case you step in a lily pond in the wide conservatory or walk into the shiny suit of armor that appears in different places each day.

The stairs wind down until you meet up with the rest of the house. Here is where you usually face your first choice for the day. This morning a wide corridor with arched ceilings stretches off to the left and right. Embroidered tapestries hang along the oak paneled walls.

To your left, the corridor ends abruptly. A suit of armor stands at the dead end, its bright metallic form leaning slightly forward, its gauntlet holding up the edge of the last tapestry. Behind it you glimpse the corner of a small door. You wouldn't expect a kitchen behind there.

To your right, the corridor is blocked by an impassable hole in the floor with a ladder poking out. The carpet is ripped and torn around the hole as though a bomb has gone off in the night. That's weird. You didn't hear an explosion.

You're not confident the kitchen would be down there either. There are no other options.

It's time to make your first decision of the day. Do you:

Climb down the hole? **P32**

Or

Look behind the secret door? **P5**

Take the secret door behind the suit of armor

The Magician doesn't leave notes, but he does leave signs. The door behind the tapestry is an invitation, and you're going to accept it. You take a good look at the tapestry before you go behind it. You want to remember the picture so you can recognize it again. The picture isn't one of the most interesting in the Magician's house — many are embroidered with scenes of fantastic creatures. This is just a dense forest with the roof of a tower peeking out of it.

The armor appears in different places in the Magician's house all the time. You bumped into it last week when you were carrying a large flower display. It was standing in the middle of the ballroom as if it were about to dance. Another time, you found it in the garden under a tree. You've looked before, but there's nobody inside.

Today, the armor has a leather pouch swinging from one gauntlet. Maybe there's something handy inside. You open the pouch and find a jar. The glass is warm in your hand, and a faded handwritten label reads: *sunshine*. There's a faint yellow swirl moving inside. You decide to take the jar with you.

Now you examine the door.

The door behind the tapestry is set into the wall, so when the cloth covered it, there were no bumps that would have made you think something was behind it. There's a creak as you open the door stiffly inwards. Now you blink into a dark passage. It probably travels between other rooms in the house — big old houses have them so guests can move about in the grand spaces and servants can bustle in between without disturbing them. Who knows, maybe you've found a speedier way to the kitchen?

As you step inside, you hear a plop. The red frog lands in front of you.

"Coming along to explore, are you?"

The red frog looks up at you with big eyes. It can probably see quite well in the dark, but you can't.

Fearing you will tread on the little amphibian, you bend and scoop it up. It feels warm in your hand. It makes a couple of leaps up your arm and then snuggles itself on your shoulder.

You treat each new part of the Magician's house like you're walking on thin ice. You keep your back foot ready to take your weight should reality give way. The Magician's house swirls with dreams that pool in corners of rooms and cluster on carpets like other houses attract dust. It's not the usual way for a house to behave.

Behind you the door clicks shut and it is utterly dark. You hear clanking as the suit of armor resumes its position in front of the tapestry, and a swish as it drops the tapestry back over the doorway. Oh well, it isn't as if anyone would come looking for you anyway. You shudder when you think about being trapped in here forever. Don't be stupid, you remind yourself. You know better than to get frightened in this passage. You might as well feel like that in the whole house!

Now, where are we going?

As your eyes try to make sense of the darkness, your feet slowly feel their way forward, but there doesn't seem to be anything to trip on. You can smell dust in the air. The leather pouch, slung over your shoulder, feels warm. You take another peek inside the pouch — the jar is quite visible. Sunshine, eh? You take out the jar and unscrew the lid a tiny bit. Soft yellow light swirls out like smoke. As the light spreads you can see more and more of the passage. Not knowing how much light you have, or how much you'll need, you put the lid back on. Now you can see quite well and resume cautious exploration.

A cool draft to your right draws your eye to a part of the wall where the paneling is different. At eye level is a square of board about the size of a large book with a hinge at one end. It's a little window of some sort. You open it and find yourself staring into a room you've seen before. It's the Magician's drawing room and has high ceilings and long portraits hanging from every wall.

It is time to make a decision.

Do you:

Investigate the drawing room? **P8**

Or

Go down the secret passage? **P12**

Investigate the Magician's drawing room.

The drawing room is octagonal. It has a carved door in one wall and paintings on all the rest. The Magician is shown in every painting.

The one closest to the door shows him performing in a theatre. He's dressed in purple robes and a pointy hat and is making a great glass orb float in the air.

The next painting shows the Magician sawing a long box in half — there is a person's head at one end and their feet at the other. Another painting shows the Magician making potions, and in another he wears shiny armor and stands next to a dragon.

The pictures are bemusing. Although you recognize the Magician in each one, you can't recall what he looks like when you look away. You never seem to be able to remember exactly what the Magician looks like, even though you have breakfast with him most mornings. It's the same with these paintings. You can remember details like the clothes he is wearing and other people and things in the picture, but when you look away, you can't bring the Magician's face to your mind.

The red frog climbs up from your shoulder and jumps on your head. It is looking too.

There is a table in the center of the room. On top of the table is a round woven basket, shaped almost like a ball. The basket has a woven lid. As you watch it, the basket gives an almost imperceptible shudder. You wonder what is inside.

The frog on your head gives a little twitch, perhaps wanting you to move on. Then the basket gives a little twitch too. What is in there?

By the light of the sunshine jar, you see a catch in the wall. You lift the catch and a panel swings open. You step inside the room, curious about what is inside the basket.

You cross the room and take a quick peek out of the far door. Hooray! The kitchen door is only a short distance down the hallway. You put the frog down and leave the door open so the way to the kitchen will be more likely to stay put. You'll only be a minute and then you can get straight to breakfast.

Now, back to the basket. What could be making it move? It shudders and shakes as you get nearer and then, as you reach out, goes perfectly still.

You'll open and shut the lid fast to see what is inside. You'll just take a quick peek.

You count out loud: "One, two, three!"

The snake in the basket is very fast. Before you blink, it has sunk its fangs into your wrist and then disappeared back into the basket. The lid drops back on the top. A cold heaviness spreads up your arm from the bite. You watch as your hand and arm turn to stone as the poison spreads further. Before you can run to the door, your whole body becomes heavy and everything slows down.

Staring across the room, you see another picture of the Magician. He has a flute and is charming a snake out of a basket, the same basket that is on the table, the same snake that bit you. The Magician's eyes are laughing.

Sometime later, you hear people coming into the room. Being a statue, you can't turn to see who is there, and the voices are muffled. The snake's bite has dulled your senses. Eventually, the gardeners arrive and tip you up into a wheelbarrow. They move you outside by the topiary and fountains. You watch the moon getting full and then turning into a small crescent again. Some nights, strange creatures come into the Magician's garden. If you ever change back, you'd like to find out more about them. There is a lot of time to think. What would have happened if you hadn't opened the basket but had turned back and kept going down the passage? If you ever come back to life, you'd like to find out. From time to time, the red frog comes and sits beside you.

You finally come back to life during a lightning storm. Wet and cold, you head indoors and find your way back to your room in the turret.

Maybe someone else will have moved in? To your relief, it still looks like your room. In the morning, you are incredibly hungry and vow to yourself NOT to get distracted on the way to breakfast in the future.

At breakfast everyone greets you like a long-lost friend and asks what it was like to be turned to stone.

After breakfast you go out to see where you had been standing in the garden and see that your footprints are still clearly visible on the ground. You must have been standing there for months.

It is time to make a decision. Do you

Return to your room in the turret and start over again? **P1**

Or

Go back to the secret passage? **P15**

You have decided to go down the secret passage.

A faint breeze alerts you to the possibility of another door in the passage. On one side of the hall, the wall is made of blackboard canvas with upside down writing and numbers on it and some sort of map. Why is the writing upside down? Hang on — some of this writing is familiar. This is the back of the big roller blackboard in the Magician's classroom.

The schoolroom must be on the other side of the wall. When the board is rolled forward, the writing on this side will be upside down.

Yesterday, in the schoolroom, you were asking how long it took to sail to the other side of the world. Miss Eleanor Spurlock, the teacher, drew a quick map of Australia as she answered the question. You remember her drawing the southern continent now. That island you are looking at is Australia, but you didn't recognize it upside down.

The giant blackboard takes up half of one of the schoolroom walls. There is a rope and pulley to turn the blackboard — when you pull the rope, the whole board rotates like a giant flat wheel revealing a new expanse of board for Miss Spurlock to draw on. Sometimes she asks you or one of your classmates to turn the board. Turning the crank is fun, but what is also interesting are the pictures that are sometimes revealed in a new stretch of blackboard canvas. Once, a large portrait of a tiger appeared and nobody had the heart to erase it, so everything was written around it that day. Later, when you looked for the tiger again, it wasn't there. Another time, a large sailing ship was revealed with a sailor leaning over the side to see a mermaid. Again, everyone agreed to leave the picture, and next time it came around, you saw that the ship was leaving. The man now had a tail, and he was swimming off with the mermaid.

Further down the secret passage, you hear someone crying through the walls. You recognize the back of a large painting with a spy hole within it. You open the sunshine jar a tiny bit so you have more light. This section of the passage is quite different from the rest. It is all made of wood, and parts almost look as if it has grown here rather than been built. The back of the picture seems very organic. It has a glossy wooden frame, which seems odd considering this is the back of the picture and nobody would be viewing it from this side.

When you slide the panel open you are looking into a circular room a little bigger than your own turret. There is a wooden bed with blue and green embroidered sheets and coverlet. It looks somehow as if it grew in the room as the base of the bed seems to have roots that sink into the wooden floor. A girl is thumping the pillows on the bed. A mirror leaning against one wall reflects the picture you stand behind. It is a picture of Medusa — the woman who had snakes instead of hair. You have seen her in a book about mythology. The rest of the room contains a chest and a small book case and a table and chair. There is an ornate window with a seat built under it and some sort of weaving frame.

The crying girl rolls across the bed and then pushes herself up and over to the dressing table. She is wearing a green velvet dress. Her long black hair is arranged in raven ringlets. She angrily wipes her eyes and reaches for a book. You see she has a stack of them. You love books and you peer to see what kind they are, but the next thing you see is that she hurls the top one against the window. You brace yourself, thinking the window will smash, but the book just bounces off it and slaps to the floor. She sighs and opens another one up and starts reading.

She seems so despondent.

You let more sunshine out of the jar to see the picture you stand behind. You see it is in fact a door set into the wall. There is wooden handle on the picture and, just like the bed, the handle seems to have grown there like a branch.

Should you open the door or continue down the passage?

It is time to make a decision. Do you:

Continue down the secret passage? **P15**

Or

Open the door? **P19**

You have decided to continue down the passageway.

You have a nagging feeling you missed out on something, but breakfast is the most important thing on your mind. You head on down the corridor, and soon there is another little door just like the first one you entered. Hopefully, the kitchen is on the other side.

The passage door opens into a large pot cupboard and, with a clatter, you crawl out through pans and tins into the kitchen. As you open the door, you smell reassuring breakfast smells. Your homing instincts have done it again.

The kitchen is the anchor of the whole house. It is more solid and reliable and, of course, it is where the food is. To call it simply 'the kitchen' just doesn't do it justice. It is a vast area with three different fireplaces, multiple ovens, and work tables. Over to the right are two wooden doors which lead to the pantries and the herbarium. They are always there — they don't move around. Over to the left a door takes you to the sun room and on to the cook's quarters. The sun room looks out to the garden and even when it's night time it looks like day through its windows. The gardeners sit there in the evenings sometimes to look for slugs with their slug nets.

The floor is made of flagstones. They are great grey slabs of stone sunk into the ground. They were once flat but over time they have acquired slight dips where they have been smoothed by many feet. The passage of time has served to form comforting paths that ease the way for someone burdened by a tray of empty glasses or piping hot pies.

The kitchen is a deep room — the walls either side of the cupboard you crawled out of are covered in shelves and more cupboards containing plates and pots and saucepans of burnished copper.

The other side of the kitchen is set with benches running from one end to the other. The wall immediately above the benches is set with a crazy collection of different tiles — yellow and cerulean and violet and black and white with blue pictures. Above those are wide windows that go to the ceiling. From wherever you are in the kitchens you can look out to the gardens. Above your head hang is a jungle of herbs, strings of onions, and braids of garlic. There are hooks holding jugs and copper pots. Sometimes a pair of eyes peeks from a pot.

The kitchen is warm when snow covers the garden outside and cool when summer is at its height. At the stove your friend Henry is frying bacon and sausages. Mrs. Noogles turns to you and smiles.

"You've made good time this morning — come and help with these potato cakes."

You make haste to help her at the griddle, and when they are all cooked and piled in a golden pyramid, you take them to the table. The rest of the household are turning up now — some come through doors and others in stranger ways than you arrived. Scarlet, the housemaid, marches up from steps that materialize from a large flagstone in the floor. The librarian reads herself in, nose in a cookbook.

Last to arrive is the Magician. He folds himself into the room and smiles at everyone in morning greeting. The gardeners lift their caps to him, and Scarlet makes a quick bob. You are putting the last of the cutlery on the table, so you nod and he nods right back.

"Get yourselves seated!" commands Mrs. Noogles and everybody does. You know that in most great houses the master would eat on his own — never with the servants and never in the kitchen. But the Magician is not like most masters.

Everyone makes quick work of breakfast. You eat heartily and, like most of your colleagues, you put a few snacks aside for later. If you have trouble finding the kitchen, you won't go hungry.

Henry, your friend, has found a strange boy called Charlie in the house. Mrs. Noogles cleaned him up and invited him to breakfast and the Magician seems to have taken a shine to him. He invites him to join you all. You're pleased — Charlie seems like fun. He's heading out to grab his gear and asks if you want to go with him. You're considering whether you will when Mrs. Noogles says you only have two options:

Do a few tasks in the herb room and then get to school, or polish the suit of armor — which might take a while.

It is time to make a decision. Do you:

Help with the herbs? **P45**

Or

Polish the armor? **P18**

18

You have decided to polish the armor

Mrs. Noogles shows you to the armory. You had no idea there was an armory. She taps on a flagstone, and the stone rumbles beneath the rest of the floor to form a first step. Down forty more steps you find a large bench set up with clothes and oil and screw-drivers and hammers. There is not one but three suits of armor waiting patiently by the bench as if they were queuing to get their library books issued, or to buy something in a shop. So that's why you see the suit of armor everywhere — there are lots!

"Goodness! It's been a while since we did some polishing. Looks like the job has been piling up," says Mrs. Noogles.

She points out what needs to be done. Each suit must be dismantled and each piece polished and oiled. You'll be lucky to be out of here by dinner. Oh well, you think, better get started, it's not always an exciting day in the Magician's house.

You have just finished the first one when you look up and find a fourth has arrived. This could be a really long day.

It's time to make a decision. Do you:

See Mrs. Noogles about another task instead? **P45**

Or

Start at the beginning of the story and try another path? **P1**

You have decided to open the door

The picture door creaks open stiffly. As you step into the room, you smell clean fresh air and the scent of pine trees. The girl whirls towards you in surprise. She grabs a book as if she will throw it at you, and you duck in case she does. Then she puts down the book and smiles as she works out you aren't a threat.

You introduce yourself. As you do, the red frog jumps down to the floor with a plop.

"Nice frog. Is it enchanted? What can it do?"

Now that she mentions it, you suppose the frog probably *is* enchanted in some way, but you explain you have never seen it do anything useful or even interesting. It's just a frog.

"Have you tried kissing it? They do that in stories, you know."

You both look at the frog, but neither of you think this is a good time to try kissing it. The girl introduces herself as Devorah. You decide to ask what the problem is — you explain how you accidentally ended up spying on her on your way to breakfast.

"It wasn't on purpose — I was on my way to the kitchen and I found the secret passage and then…"

Devorah cuts your apology off:

"It's perfectly fine. I'm so happy to have someone to talk to! Perhaps this means I can get out of the passage too!"

While she's talking, you look around the room. It's high up in a tower and much bigger than your own turret. There is no staircase, so you wonder how Devorah gets outside. Her home is less like a building and more like being inside a giant tree. Near the picture doorway you entered is a large balcony. The view is completely different from your bedroom. Instead of seeing London, a great forest stretches out as far as you can see. You are far from the Magician's house. At the foot of the tower, great roots anchor it to the forest floor as though it grew there. It's a dizzyingly long way down, and the surrounding trees are not close enough to jump to. You can see a rough road starts at the foot of the tower and disappears into the forest. Here and there, the road appears again on the hills off in the distance. At the top of one hill, you see a small thatched hut. Other than that, the tower is alone in a sea of trees.

Devorah calls you back into the room.

"Be careful out there — she might see you!"

"Who?"

"The witch, Baba Yaga."

"What a funny name," you say. "I've never heard of Baba Yaga."

"How can you not know her? She torments the country."

"I'm not from this country. I am from a magic house, though."

Devorah nods and doesn't seem too surprised.

"Your Magician's house has connected to a very different part of the world."

Devorah explains she has been imprisoned in this tower for months.

"It was winter time when I came here and now it's nearly winter again. My father, the king stood up to Baba Yaga. She arrived in her house that moves on chicken feet, and she took me away. I thought she would eat me, but she locked me up here. I suppose my father will do what she wants with me imprisoned. And worse, when she visits me she talks about her son all the time. I think she wants me to marry him."

Devorah shudders, thinking about Baba Yaga's son. Then she grins in a brave way and leans in to whisper, "I've been trying to steal a little of her magic each time she visits — just a tiny amount when she climbs in the window and won't notice. Her magic is very strong. I'm using it to try to escape using the picture you came through."

Devorah has only recently been able to come through the picture doorway but hasn't yet been able to cross over to the Magician's house.

You ask why the witch climbs in the window and doesn't use the door.

"There is no door. This is an enchanted tower." Devorah looks at you like you don't know anything. You don't know much, but this story is reminding you of a tale about a girl with long, long hair. Maybe that's where this witch, Baba Yaga, got the idea from.

"How do you steal her magic?" you ask.

Devorah looks ashamed. "I know it's not very nice to use other people's magic, but I need to get out of here. I thought if I made a magical door, I might be able to escape."

Devorah tells you she steals magic from the witch by plucking one of her hairs as she helps haul her in the window.

"That's very clever," you say, and Devorah smiles.

"I learned a little magic from my great-great-aunt who lives outside my father's castle. She taught me how to weave rogue magic, and that's what I've done."

Devorah shows you a fine thread of plaited hair surrounding the picture. In this way, she's charmed the picture to become a portal. You tell her you think she's been very clever.

"I've added some charms of protection as you would to a door. I was hoping it would start to act like a door, and it has! I just felt for other magic and tried to connect to it. So far, I've only managed to get a little way down the passage. You coming through might have helped strengthen the connection, I'm sure, but I think I'm going to need a little more magic to get myself through."

Devorah is keen to try to get through the passage again and into the safety of the Magician's house. You both step through the picture door and close it behind you. Back inside the corridor, you open the sunshine jar again. You head to the door you thought would take you to the kitchen.

At the end of the passage, there is a door exactly like the one you entered this morning — you have travelled in a circle and are back where you started. When you open the door the suit of armor stands there holding the tapestry up. You walk through all right, but something is wrong —

Devorah can't come through. It's as though there is a wall for her that you can't see.

"My spell isn't strong enough. I can't get through the door. You've been able to visit me, but I need a bit more magic to get through. I'll have to wait for the witch and risk taking a tiny bit more of her power."

You are nervous of Devorah getting caught by the witch stealing more magic. Maybe you could do something to help.

"Have you tried signaling to that hut you can see from your tower?" you ask.

Devorah looks alarmed.

"Hut? You saw a hut? But that's her! She travels in a hut on chicken legs. There isn't anyone else on that road and no other dwelling. That means she's coming. I have to get back before she finds what I've been doing."

Devorah hastens back down the passage to her prison. What should you do?

It is time to make a decision. Do you:

Go for help? **P29**

Or

Return with Devorah to her tower? **P24**

Return with Devorah to her tower

You follow Devorah down the passage. Behind you, the door shuts, and now the passage is in near darkness. The sunshine jar is empty.

The tower must be close by on your right. You bump into Devorah, who must be searching too, and then retch as you smell something rotten like dead meat. Devorah is trembling — she leans close and holds a finger to your lips. You don't need her to tell you that the witch is here.

The sound of the witch's voice makes your blood run cold.

"That's right, my pretty, keep quiet and let me listen to your heart, beating fast like a trapped little bird. Two trapped birds. Mmmmm, someone smells delicious. It seems you've found yourself some tasty company."

The witch is very close. You step backwards softly, wishing frantically that the Magician's house would play a trick on her so you can escape. You put your hand out to feel the wall, but instead you feel trees! Underfoot, the ground is suddenly rough and you realize the witch has transported you both back to her forest. It is dark and terrifying.

The red frog tickles at your neck. You didn't even know it was still with you. You carefully gather it and crouch down to feel for a safe place on the ground for it to sit. You might be going to meet a sticky end, but there's no need for the frog to join you. It feels very warm, perhaps trying to give you a little courage. When you stand up again, Devorah feels for your hand. You stand still and listen for the witch's approach. You can't run because you would just hit a tree in the thick forest.

Just then, Devorah taps you, and you wonder why. Then you see a red glow on the ground that is steadily getting bigger and brighter. The frog is giving off light and getting larger! It is now the size of a cat. As the light gets brighter, you start to see the shapes of trees and the forest floor — ahead you see the looming form of the tower that Devorah has spent so long trapped inside. At the base of the tower stands Baba Yaga. She is a black malevolent shape that reeks of carrion. Perhaps the frog wants to help so you can make a run for it?

Baba Yaga steps forward.

"What's this? You've found a new pet."

She looks at the frog as it glows and grows. She appears about to kick your little friend, so you throw the empty jar of sunshine at her. The witch doesn't even flinch, but she doesn't hurt the frog. Instead, she turns her gaze to look at you. Her eyes are black and merciless, and the light from the frog reveals a strangely distorted face with a wide mouth and sharp, pointed teeth.

She licks her lips, and her face twists into a horrible smile. Then she says, "Let's get the oven stoked."

She makes a cackling bird call. There is scrabbling and creaking as her enchanted hut comes into the clearing. It moves on four giant chicken legs with a drunken dancing step. The hut turns so the front door is facing you. The door opens, and you see an oven with a raging fire inside.

"Crebbit!"

The frog makes the first sound you have ever heard from it. It is now the size of a lion. It jumps between you and the house as if to say, "Don't try it."

The witch laughs, and then several things happen at once. She raises her hands to throw a spell, and the frog opens its mouth. She opens her own mouth but nothing comes out because the frog's long tongue has shot out and wrapped around her, and she is being dragged into its mouth. There is a gulp from the frog, and then its stomach glows an especially bright red like a furnace. You imagine you can hear the witch screaming, but you aren't sure because there is suddenly so much more noise. The witch's house is disintegrating, and four ordinary-looking chickens fly free from the spell that has made them carry her home. They head off into the night, squawking and flying about erratically into the forest. The tower, Devorah's prison, begins to creak and change too. The witch's magic is fading rapidly.

The picture of snaked haired Medusa, which Devorah made into a door, lands near you with a thud. It is propped against the trunk of what was once the tower but now is a very tall, but ordinary-looking tree. Light is beginning to from the sky, and you can see the forest around you.

Devorah walks toward the painting. After meeting the witch, the picture of Medusa with snakes for hair doesn't

seem too bad. You catch yourself thinking she might have been a very lonely person if everyone she met turned to stone. Devorah tries the door, and luckily it is still working.

"Quick! You had better return before the magic is gone," she says.

You try to convince her to come with you, but she shakes her head and points up the dirt road. There, in the distance, you see horses and riders approaching. Devorah waves to them.

"It's my father's men — they will take me home. This place has been hidden to them by magic, but now they've found me."

The riders carry banners and wear old-fashioned chainmail and leather helms. Large dogs run alongside the horses. You're glad they are apparently friends of hers.

Devorah throws her arms around you in a hug and then pushes you through the painting door with the red frog following. The door shuts with a clang, and you know it will never open again. You start to fumble your way along in the passage. There is a loud plopping sound, and then you see a red glow ahead at your feet. The red frog is still glowing, and it helps you find a door.

You fall out of the passage and bang into the suit of armor, which clatters to the floor of the kitchen. Most of the household are eating at a long kitchen table. Mrs. Noogles, tells you that you can clean up that suit of armor as soon as you've had something to eat. Then she sees the red frog. It is the size of a very large dog.

"What have you been feeding that frog?"

In a normal house, people might have been asking where you have been all this time, but this is the Magician's house, and people know bizarre things happen. You bet your weird morning was one of the oddest, though. The red frog hops over to the door to the garden and looks up at the door knob. You open the door and watch it hop off toward the water fountain. You wonder if you will find it back in your tower tomorrow.

Mrs. Noogles calls you to the table and you realize you are famished. You sit down and listen to the others talking. The Magician looks over to you and smiles, and you grin back.

You have reached the end of this part of the story.

Now you have another decision to make. Do you:

Start the story over again and try other paths? **P1**

Or

Consult the list of choices to find somewhere you haven't been yet? **P84**

You have decided to go for help

You watch Devorah run back to her prison. There must be something you can do. You don't think the hole in the ground will help. You need to find the Magician or someone else who knows magic. You look behind another tapestry and find a door that leads you to a balcony. There is a clanking beside you, and you turn to see the suit of armor now standing to attention at the start of an ornate flight of stairs.

You know these stairs very well. If you run down the middle, you'll take twice as long to get down them as it would if you skip down the sides. There is a party in the middle of the stairs — or the house is keeping the memory of one. If you go down the center, all you'll do is end up saying "excuse me" and "pardon me" and "it's just down the hall" to a host of tittering ladies and mustachioed men and avoiding waiters carrying trays with precariously balanced glasses.

You want to go down fast. You leap down the stairs, hugging the wall, and then hear banging and crashing in a nearby room, but you can't spare time to investigate. It can't be Devorah because she can't get through. At last, you see the kitchen door.

You burst through and find most of the household eating their breakfast. The Magician is there too making short work of a plate of sausages and other good breakfast fare. The cook, Mrs. Noogles, starts to tell you off for being so late.

It's your job to help. At the same time, you are blurting your story to everyone and repeating the message that there is a girl trapped in a tower by a witch.

"Interesting," says the Magician.

"Appalling," says Mrs. Noogles. One of the garden boys hesitantly asks whether Devorah is good-looking. You scowl at him and yell in frustration:

"I need some help here!"

There is silence after you yell, and then you hear a croaking from a pot cupboard. Mrs. Noogles opens the cupboard door and out squeezes the red frog. Everyone stares. It is now the size of a large dog. It also seems to be giving off heat and belching. The smell is not pleasant. The frog looks at you, and then hops to the garden door. It looks up at the door knob expectantly. You start to let it out when the Magician calls out, "Wait!" He crosses over and takes a good look at the frog. He opens its mouth and peers in. It doesn't smell good.

The Magician announces the frog has recently eaten something, or someone, particularly malevolent.

"Was the frog with you at this tree tower?"

You nod yes.

"Well, I suspect your new friend won't be having any more trouble from her witch. This frog is attracted to bad, and it's had a bellyful today."

The Magician turns to the cheeky gardener.

"You'd better fetch a shovel. What goes in must come out, and we'll need a pit digging for this lot. Still, it might be just the thing to start a nice crop of rhubarb."

The Magician lets the frog outside, and together you head back to the tapestry where you found the passage. There is no door anymore. How will you know for sure that Devorah is all right? Wait. The picture on the tapestry has changed.

Now you can see a road between the trees. A group of riders is heading off down its path. All but one of the riders wears armor. She has long raven hair, and has half turned back on her horse and waves at you. It is Devorah. She is going home.

She probably can't see, but, just in case, you wave back.

You have reached the end of this part of the story. Do you:

Return to the beginning of this story and try another path? **P1**

Or

Go to the list of choices and choose somewhere else to start reading from? **P84**

Go down the ladder into the hole

You hold onto the smooth wooden ends of the ladder that poke out above the floor and swing yourself onto its rungs. Clambering downwards, you hope you'll soon smell frying bacon.

You want to go to the kitchen, but you know that you can't always predict where things will be in the Magician's house. The kitchen could be found upstairs or down. There is no sense to it. In fact, most people who live in the Magician's house keep a sandwich or an apple in their pocket in case they don't see the kitchen for a while. As you think about food your stomach growls, anticipating one of Mrs. Noogles' breakfasts.

Mrs. Noogles is the cook in the house and she never wanders far from her domain. She says she has lost patience with the rest of the house. Her quarters are at the back of the kitchen. She has a sunny room with a view of the garden, a fireplace and an easy chair. You have never seen her in the chair, as she is usually bustling about.

The ladder is sturdy and well-secured so it doesn't wobble. The hole above you gets smaller as you climb downward. Tiny glowworms give enough light for you to make out what sort of a hole you've entered. You put out your hand and touch smooth cold rock and moss. In one place, there are so many glow worms that you can make out mushrooms growing on a ledge beside a cave. The cave would be great to explore when you've done your work, and had breakfast. That's assuming you ever see it again.

As you climb further down the hole, the light dims. Your eyes are open wide and straining to see between the rungs of the ladder. Suddenly, another pair of eyes opens right in front of you.

You freeze. The eyes look at you, and you look at the eyes. You hear your heart thump loudly and then, even louder, you hear the noise of your rumbling stomach. The rumble echoes through the hole. The owner of the eyes lets out a deep chuckle, and you relax at once. You are just about to ask the owner of the eyes if they think the kitchen is near when they surprise you again. Whoever it is reaches between the rungs of the ladder and pushes you off! You lose

your

grip

and

fall.

You flail uselessly but can't grip on to anything to stop your fall. But as you reach about, you realize you aren't falling that fast. It is like falling through treacle or custard. The air seems thicker than usual. You relax a little and enjoy falling for a while, there isn't anything you can really do about it, and at this speed you don't think you'll get hurt.

Just as you are starting to really enjoy the ride, it changes: you fall faster, and light rushes up underneath you. Before you can panic, you arrive with a thump that knocks the breath out of you. When you come to your senses, you see you are back on your bed in your turret room. Above, you can see a hole in the arched ceiling, except instead of seeing the morning sun through the hole, you just see darkness. You hear that chuckle again and a face pushes into your room as if parting black clouds. You recognize the large eyes, which you now see are bright green. The rest of its face is a velvety black so it is hard to see a mouth or nose or eyebrows, but it is the face of a large shaggy cat. It grins to show an impressive number of teeth.

"Hey! Why did you push me?" you ask the cat creature, not really expecting a reply. It grins again and then replies:

"To get you where you were going faster!"

The cat face disappears but then pops back a moment later.

"Don't suppose you could throw a few mice in the hole sometime? I'm getting bored with catching bats."

You stare at the hole a bit longer, but the creature has gone.

A plunking noise alerts you to the red frog. It is springing up the wall. Its little suckered feet allow it to stick where gravity wouldn't usually allow, but it's a difficult task. It hurls itself toward the hole in the ceiling, but, with each jump, gravity takes its toll and twice it falls, morphing into something made of rubber that sends it bouncing a little higher up the wall to try again. Finally, it lands just next to the hole and catches one side of it with a foot before losing its grip and landing beside you. One edge of the hole peels off the ceiling, like a pancake you once flipped too high. The frog hurls itself up the wall again and pulls another section of the hole away.

On its next attempt, the frog manages to wriggle underneath a section of the hole, which finally detaches it from the ceiling. It falls like a leaf and covers most of your bed.

The other side of the hole isn't a hole at all. The frog sits on top of it. You touch it cautiously. It is soft as silk. You fold it up so the hole is on the inside and soon it's not much bigger than a handkerchief. Thinking this hole might come in handy; you carefully put it in your pocket before you and the frog head back down the stairs.

This time when you head down the stairs, the hole has gone because it's in your pocket. You can still go behind the tapestry that the suit of armor is showing you, or you can head down a green carpeted hallway.

Which way should you go?

It is time to make a decision. Do you:

Go down the hallway? **P36**

Or

Go through the secret door behind the suit of armor? **P5**

You have decided to go down the hallway

You step carefully, hoping to find your way to breakfast. You treat the ground as if it is an icy surface — keeping your back foot ready to take your weight should reality slip away.

The Magician's house swirls with dreams that pool in corners of rooms and cluster on carpets like other houses attract dust. Although you can't remember living any other way, you know it's not a usual way for a house to behave.

Mrs. Noogles has had quite enough of the rest of the house. She is the cook and she never wanders far from her kitchen — partly that's because she is always busy concocting food and partly because she long ago lost patience with the rest of the house. She has burnt the dinner too many times being caught out in a 'dining room dream' as she calls it. She can reliably find her quarters through a door at the back of the kitchen — a large sunny room with a view of the garden, a fire place and an easy chair. She also has an area of the garden where she directs the growing of herbs and vegetables and fruit and a room where she dries herbs and stores her preserves and jams.

Actually, you quite like some of the dreams you have found in the house — but you have learned to watch your footing so you don't have to see a dream through if you don't want to. They aren't all pleasant. Finding your way through the dreams doesn't seem to be something everyone in the house can do. Mrs. Noogles looked at you strangely when you once described your 'back-foot' technique to her.

The grand staircase appears, and you nimbly miss the third step down. Treading on the third step transforms the quiet house to a crowded party with a ball going on and a host of masked people leaping about making noise, clinking glasses and talking about ridiculous things. It was good the first few times you experienced it, but it makes going down the stairs very slow because of all the times you need to say "excuse me" as you pass people and "no, thank you" as you are offered drinks and "just down the hall on the left" for the people looking for a powder room. If you do go down through the party, it all disappears when you hit the last stair.

If you are hungry, you can pick up little pies from the silver trays as they are offered around. Unfortunately, it is the sort of party where all the food is very small and you are expected to take only one thing from a tray at a time, so really it is better to push on and look for the kitchen.

You slide down the last half of the banister, feeling pretty pleased with your start to the day. Ahead, the kitchen door is open at the end of the corridor, and there are pleasant cooking smells wafting toward you. You veer to the left to avoid a dream of walking through a summer field after a sun shower. It is always annoying to get wet feet. You are just passing the last door when you hear a huge thump and somebody cries out. You are so close to breakfast!

What do you do? Do you:

Find out what made the noise behind the door? **P38**

Or

Ignore the noise and head down the passageway? **P15**

YOU SAY WHICH WAY

Find out what made the noise behind the door

You open the door cautiously and immediately let out a sneeze. The room is swirling with soot from the chimney. A small person sits near the hearth, rubbing their head. They are so covered in soot that they are almost completely black — except for the whites of their eyes which look up at you in fear. It's a chimney sweep. You have seen them before on London's streets, making their way through the city. You've never seen one up close before, though.

"Please, I lost my way, and I'm in ever so much trouble. I didn't mean to cause a mess."

The sweep seems so scared, and you wonder if he is hurt. You can't imagine how he could have been cleaning in the Magician's chimneys. You know for a fact the Magician sends a pair of enchanted squirrels through there every second Wednesday, so he doesn't need a sweep.

"Cheer up. You won't be in trouble," you say. "I was just about to get some breakfast. Are you peckish? If you want to eat, come with me. I can help you find the front door after that if you like."

The sweep smiles and nods. He looks down at himself and is clearly wondering how he should proceed because with every step he will make a sooty footprint.

"Don't worry," you say, "there're a lot of cleaners here." You don't mention you haven't seen them yourself, but someone or something straightens up round here all the time. "We'll get you seen to."

You step back in the hall, and he follows. You have just shut the door when the sweep suddenly exclaims:

"My brush!"

He opens the door again and stops stock still. The room is completely clean — the only evidence he has ever been there is his brush sitting at attention by the fireplace.

"See," you say, "they're very fast. Now let's make haste before we miss breakfast."

The sweep is astounded that a sooty room with no other door has been cleaned so fast, and he enters the room cautiously to collect his brush. As he leaves, he bends to look under the furniture as if maids with dusters and brooms might be hiding there. You take his hand and carefully negotiate the last few steps to the kitchen.

When the sweep sees the kitchen, he stops and stares. The kitchen is like the anchor of the whole house. Somehow it is more solid and reliable and, of course, it is where the food is. To call it simply the kitchen just doesn't do it justice. It is a vast area with three different fireplaces, multiple ovens, and work tables. To the right are two wooden doors that lead to the cool store and the herbarium. To the left, a door takes you to the sun room and on to Mrs. Noogles' quarters. The sunroom is sunny and you can see the garden as if its day, even when it's night, through its windows.

The kitchen floor is made of flagstones, great squares of stone that remind you of a giant's chess board. They were once probably flat, but over time they have acquired slight dips and been smoothed by many feet.

The walls are covered in shelves containing plates and pots and saucepans of burnished copper. The other side of the kitchen has a bench running from one end to the other. The wall above the bench is set with a crazy collection of different tiles — yellow and cerulean and violet and black and white with blue pictures. Above the rows of tiles are wide windows that go all the way to the ceiling. From wherever you are in the kitchens, you can look out to the gardens.

Your friend Henry is frying bacon and sausages. He grins at you and nods to the sweep and then gets back to his task.

"What manner of mess do we have here?" Mrs. Noogles says, as she emerges from the cool store. She sets down the potatoes she was fetching, puts out a grater and a bowl and points at you.

Mmmm, potato cakes, you think. You know what to do and set to grating the potatoes. Mrs. Noogles takes charge of the sweep.

"We'll need hot water and soap."

From above her head, she reaches for a large tin tub. At that moment, Scarlet, the housemaid, comes into the room. She is yawning and stretching and about to start her day too. Mrs. Noogles sends her up to the servants' wardrobe to find some clothes for the sweep and then sets the tub into an alcove. She bustles about fetching kettles of hot water and raps on the window to attract the attention of a passing gardener. He comes in with more water from the pump, which she adds to the steaming bath.

The sweep stands about surveying the kitchen and being careful not to let soot fall in the way. He eyes the bath warily but is clearly interested in the food you are preparing. Lastly, Mrs. Noogles directs you to fetch a screen from the storeroom, and then she and the sweep disappear behind it, and there is a splashing sound as the sweep is immersed in water and given a good soaping. Mrs. Noogles lets out a steady stream of instructions to you and Henry from behind the screen.

You put the potato cakes onto the griddle and start making the toast. The sweep keeps up his chatter.

"I won't half be in trouble, Mrs. Noogles, if I don't get out and find my boss."

You think he is probably relishing the chance to get clean and looking forward to the prospect of a hot breakfast.

Scarlet returns with towels, britches, a shirt, and some shoes. There are all sorts in the storerooms including fancy dress. You are fairly sure Scarlett was wearing a different pair of shoes earlier. Mrs. Noogles comes from behind the screen and gathers them up and then leaves the sweep to get dressed. She plunges herself into plating up bacon and sausages and the potato cakes you and Henry have prepared. You have buttered the toast, and now you set about wiping down the table and setting out places for everyone in the household.

"I think Himself will be coming for his breakfast this morning, so let's lay a few extra places."

How Mrs. Noogles knows this, you can't guess. 'Himself'

is the name she uses for the Magician. You know from talking to other servants in the alley that it isn't usual for a master to eat with the household staff, but the Magician isn't usual and neither is the house. It isn't usual for the staff to go to school, but a schoolroom presents itself from time to time, and no matter how much you've tried to avoid it, the doors all seem to open onto lessons in a determined way.

The sweep rounds the screen and looks a perfectly ordinary person now he is not covered in soot. You are about to usher him to the table when every door to the kitchen opens at once — two gardeners enter from outside, stamping their feet to avoid dirt coming onto the floor, Murphy the butler arrives from another door, and the teacher comes through a cupboard door. The Magician arrives at the table without the need of a door. One moment he wasn't there, and the next he sort of folds himself into the space.

"A particularly fine morning, Mrs. Noogles," says the Magician. "Sit, lad."

He points the sweep to a seat at the long table. The gardeners don't need telling, and sit themselves down as fast as if they were playing musical chairs. Soon everyone except Mrs. Noogles and you are seated as you plunk down plates and knives and forks and toast before helping to carry over platters of potato cakes and bacon and a great dish of scrambled eggs and fried tomatoes. As soon as the Magician raises a fork to his mouth everyone else follows.

"I think we'd like to know your name, young man," states

the Magician.

"Mmmf mmmfh, I'm Charlie," says the sweep through a mouthful of food.

"He came down the chimney," you add, though you suspect the Magician knows this already. He knows most things that happen in the house.

The Magician nods and continues to ask Charlie questions. Charlie explains that his father earned less money than his family spent.

"The result of earning *more* than you spend is happiness, but the result of earning *less* than you spend is ruin," Charlie says. "Well, that's what my muvver said when they were taking all our furniture away."

Now Charlie's family is in debtor's prison, and he works in a blacking factory.

"I glue the labels on the pots. Night times, I stay in an attic, with other boys like me. One of them told me about sweeping. I thought it might be better than gluing. It's not, though. I got turned around in the dark and was lost. I fell and I heard them on the rooftops looking for me. I called out, and the guv'ner said I was lost too far down and just to leave me. And that's what they did."

You shudder at the cruelty of leaving Charlie like that.

"What are you going to do now?" you ask.

"Tomorrow, I'm going back to the blacking factory. It pays my way. Maybe soon my father will be out of prison and I can go back to school."

"You like school?" The Magician perks up. You aren't so

excited by this topic. You were hoping the events of this morning might delay school.

"Charlie," says the Magician, "how would you like to work for me for a while? I could use another assistant at the theatre where I work. You can room here with the other staff and, if you'd like, you can attend the schoolroom with the others."

Charlie grins and nods and thanks the Magician for his offer. He turns and grins at you.

"Thank you so much for bringing me here!"

You are a little embarrassed because you have only brought him a few doors down the corridor, but you can see your actions have perhaps changed his life for the better, and that makes you feel really good.

Charlie will be fun to have around, and maybe you'll get to go with him to the theatre. You've been once or twice to deliver the Magician's equipment and to guard it from prying eyes.

Charlie needs to go and get his things from the attic where he stays. He asks if you want to tag along.

It is time to make a decision. Do you:

Go with Charlie to get his things? **P61**

Or

Don't go with Charlie? **P45**

Suddenly, Mrs. Noogles is calling

She wants you to clean up after breakfast. You take the scraps out to the hen house, and when you return Henry is whistling as he washes the dishes. You join him drying the plates, and then Mrs. Noogles gets you to work on her herbs. This is something you really like doing.

Mrs Noogles has all sorts of dried plants that she uses for cooking and medicine. You are gradually learning a lot about the process. This morning, there are herbs to hang up to dry and others to take down. Sometimes, your job is wrapping muslin over flower heads to collect the seeds. Every job has a different smell to it. You package up mustard seeds set aside from the other day and offer to take them back into the storeroom before you head to the library.

The storeroom is one of your favorite rooms. It smells of thyme and cumin and paprika and other good things for cooking. At the back of the room, are shelves of jams and pickles, and once you found a whole tin of jam tarts and you went back to the kitchen with one less in the tin. You look at the shelves now and notice a little tube with writing on it. *Hope.*

You have to reach high up to store the mustard seeds and, unbeknownst to you, the little tube falls in your pocket.

The library is another of your favorite rooms, and it's where you left your homework yesterday. That's your next destination. You've discovered a pretty good way to get there: carry a book. You learned the trick from Hannah, one of the librarians, who you noticed takes a book with her whenever she returns there. It isn't unusual for a librarian to carry a book, but the way she carried it was unusual. It was like an explorer with a compass. The rooms of the house are never short of books. The kitchen has cookery books, of course, but you wouldn't want to take one of those and get Mrs. Noogles annoyed. But over at the end of the benches is a room between the kitchen and the greenhouse. It is a small sunny space where the gardeners sometimes meet and talk. Mrs. Noogles can pass them a plate of biscuits and they can hand over bunches of carrots or new potatoes without taking off their boots. It's called the mud room because it's often filled with muddy boots, but that's only one side. There's also a wooden table and old comfy chairs and the thing you've come for, a book shelf.

You don't need to read the book that will help get you to the library, but you can't help scanning the titles. There is one about the history of roses — hmm, clearly a gardener's choice and so are many of the others, but this one seems out of place: *A Baroness Instructs the Genteel Art of Dance.* Huh! Nobody is going to miss that. You pull it out and cross through the kitchen. You don't think too hard about the library but step out into the corridor holding the book out a little ahead and let it make the choices about the direction you take.

The first room you enter is the ballroom. You step round a corner and there it is, and when you turn back, the way you came has gone. In fact, you are now standing in the middle of the ballroom. Arriving like this makes some people dizzy, but you've had it happen before so you stay on your feet.

The last time you were in the ballroom, you were helping at the Magician's winter solstice ball. It was a strange and wonderful affair. Guests were arriving for days, and the Magician erected extra towers in the garden for them to stay in — rather like some people put up tents. It was hard to know the difference between guests and entertainers, as many of the Magician's friends are also entertainers.

There were jugglers and lion tamers and trapeze artists and illusionists. There were also a couple from America who were crack shots with pistols and a number of fortune tellers and musicians. The days before they arrived were spent dusting the dreams from the house — Scarlet, Henry and you were set to work using brooms with pillow cases tied onto their ends herding them into wardrobes and placing signs on their doors such as 'do not enter' – but still some people did. Some went inside for fun (the picking strawberries dream in winter was quite entertaining) while others went in because they did not seem to think the signs applied to them.

The pistol shooting man didn't think signs were meant for him. His name was Wild Bill, and he strode into a cupboard on the first day he arrived and did not come out again until three days later. His partner didn't seem to mind and spent most of her time with a snake charmer who could tell the most entertaining stories. When the pistol shooter returned, she had already developed a new act with snakes. She claimed they were good to work with because they were deaf, unlike the other animals they'd tried to work with over the years who were unnerved by pistol shots and whip cracks.

The last night of the get-together was solstice night — the longest night of winter. The Magician said it was the night winter cracked and spring got in under ice and snow and began to send out green shoots and warmth under the earth. There was feasting and merriment and lots of dancing. The Magician had walked out onto the ballroom floor first with Mrs. Noogles. She wore a dress with the colors of autumn leaves and as she danced the dress became the colors of spring.

The ballroom is deserted now after the hectic days and nights of the solstice ball, and your feet echo as you cross the parquet floor made from small blocks of wood laid in an intricate scene. Without people all over it, you can see it is a mosaic of a forest. There are trees all around the outside of the room, and in the middle there is a party going on with tall regal people and other creatures — half men and half goats — dancing and playing flutes. There are a group of girls dancing in a circle with the goat men. At the edge of the party, looking quite out of place, you see what looks like one of the young gardeners who works for the Magician. Come to think of it, you haven't seen him since the solstice party. You stare at the picture on the floor. Is the gardener trapped in the mosaic? Is the picture somehow real?

In your hand, the book seems to gently tug at you, and you remember you were heading to the library. You feel strange walking over the floor. It's like the feeling you have in a graveyard where you don't need to be told to keep to the path. You take care not to tread on the animals and people as you make your way across the room. There are several doors in the far wall — all big and imposing. The book tugs you toward the one on the left. The suit of armor is standing beside it. Was it there before? You were quite busy looking at the floor, so you can't say for sure.

You open the door and have a moment of pride. The book has acted like a compass steering you toward the mass of books and manuscripts the Magician has stored. On the other side of the door is the library. It is a cavernous expanse of tables and shelves and cabinets with treasures from the Magician's travels.

"Don't shut that door!" a voice calls out from behind stacks of books on a table.

Then out from behind the stack comes Hannah, the librarian.

"From the sound of your footsteps, you were on a flat wooden floor. Leave the door open so I can move some of these books out to be sorted. That door has opened straight onto a flight of stairs for two days, which was absolutely useless for sorting!"

You hold open the door as the librarian bustles over and wedges a wooden triangle underneath it. Then she pulls a velvet curtain rope from her pocket and secures the door handle to a hook at the end of a shelf for good measure.

Looking up, she explains. "I wouldn't want to lose my new stock somewhere in the house if the door shut. You never know when the house is going to shuffle around."

You nod in agreement and are about to go and grab your homework when you wonder if Hannah will know whether the gardener is in any trouble. You offer to push the trolley of books she is now loading up from the table. When you get closer, you notice they smell vaguely of smoke and one or two are singed at the edges.

Hannah sees you pick one up and sniff it and offers up an explanation: "Fire rescue. There are some rare volumes here. I want to air them out and check them over for my catalogue."

Hannah goes back for more books. She returns pushing another trolley. The smell of smoke is profound even in the large ballroom. You look down at the floor to find the gardener — he isn't where you remember him. There is still a party scene with music and dancing and strange creatures, half goats and half men. You can't be sure if they have moved. Hannah notices you staring at the floor and comes over to take a look.

"Those are satyrs," she says.

"The picture on the floor has changed," you tell her. You explain how earlier you saw the gardener and now you don't.

Hannah is instantly interested. She studies the floor more intently and, like you, takes care not to walk on the creatures beneath your feet.

Suddenly, she calls out. "Is this your man?"

"That's him," you reply.

The gardener has climbed a tree. You notice something else. A wolf. You are sure you didn't see it before, and it is approaching the reveling group. A long tongue lolls from its mouth, and it appears to be very large.

Hannah springs into action and races back inside the library declaring: "We must rescue him at once!"

She returns wearing a cape with a hood, carrying a woven basket.

"Well," she says, "are you coming?"

You wonder how you'll enter the floor scene and how you'll rescue the gardener, but you follow Hannah as she begins a circuitous sort of half dance, gesturing to you to do the same. As you follow her path, it begins to make some sense. Her footsteps wind between the trees and other motifs set into the floor. In time, the ballroom floor softens between your feet, you begin to scuff up dirt, then leaves and small twigs. Looking up, you see that the ballroom walls are now decorated with a forest scene on the wallpaper. The smell of burnt books gradually fades and is replaced by the pleasant smell of damp earth after it has rained.

Before long, you duck to avoid a branch, and when you look around, there is no sign of the ballroom at all. Hannah moves along stealthily. From her basket she draws a dagger and tucks it into her belt. She also brings out a bar of chocolate and breaks a piece off.

"While we are down here it would be best if you don't eat

anything from this forest — do you understand? This type of enchantment often works by binding you with food and drink."

You nod and start to think back on the breakfast chats where the librarians have been describing their acquisition activities. You'd assumed they would be (you blush a little) boring. But the way Hannah has jumped into this mission makes you think you have completely underrated her job. Just then, you hear a howl in the distance. Hannah slows and cocks her head to listen. She signals for you to hold still. Slowly she takes off her cloak and turns it around — inside it is the color of blood.

"I'm going to scout ahead. Walk toward the sound of music and keep out of sight. See if you can find the gardener. You'll see my cloak when I want you to."

"But won't the wolf see you?"

"Wolves are color-blind, but they smell and hear better than we do. Anyway, I'm not convinced that the wolf is our greatest enemy here. I'll be back soon."

She flips the hood of her cloak over her head and vanishes, apart from her basket, which winks out of sight as it disappears under the folds of the cloak.

You head on through the woods, scrunching leaves underfoot as you move between the trees. You don't know if you are following a path or just places where the trees are not too close together. You come to a clearing and notice a strange thing. Over to your right, a tree is bursting into pink and white spring buds, but the path by which you entered the glade is covered in orange, brown and red fallen leaves. There are patches of snow to your left, but ahead the trees hold ripe summer fruit. This place has all the seasons going on at once. You walk across the clearing to a peach tree laden with perfect golden fruit. The air, as you get closer, is heavy with the sweet fruity scent. You are about to reach out and pick one when a voice from above calls out.

"I wouldn't if I were you!"

Up in another tree is the gardener. His smile broadens in recognition when he sees you, and he jumps down to clap your back and jump around.

"You've come from the Magician's house!"

You tell him how you saw him in the floor and followed a path till it turned into the forest. You ask his name, and he tells you he is Ted. As soon as Ted speaks his name, you remember him clearly, which makes you worry there might be some sort of forgetting spell involved in this adventure.

"How long have I been down here?" Ted asks. "Is the solstice party still going?"

You explain it's been quite a while since the Magician's annual party. And then you wonder:

"Have you eaten anything?"

Ted shakes his head.

"I'm not sure, but places like this usually have enchanted food. Look around, its summer and winter and spring all at once. Whatever grows here is grown with the aid of magic. The Magician has rules for us gardeners: we grow things in season and there's only a little magic around the edges –

keeping the bugs away and helping plants find the light and grow deep roots, but the food we eat is nourished by the land and not magic. This here is something different."

Then the gardener looks at you expectantly. "I don't suppose you brought any food, did you?"

In fact, you do have something you saved from breakfast — everyone keeps a snack in their pocket if they work in the Magician's house. You pull out a crumbling piece of toast, and the gardener looks at it as though it is a three course meal on silver trays. He is about to take a corner before asking:

"Do you know how to get out of here?"

You tell him you don't know, but before he can be too disappointed, you tell him about the librarian. "She'll know what to do or else there will be three of us missing, and surely the Magician will come looking with three staff lost in the house!"

Ted nods. Just then, a howl sounds very close by, and Ted invites you to climb up into the tree he came down from. You find he has made a platform up there — a number of slender branches and stems have been woven across some central ones to form something like a large hammock. He has other things up there too, and he's also woven a set of stairs to a higher platform.

You have only just climbed up when you hear paws padding into the glade, and you know the wolf is below. There is a sniffing and snuffling under your tree. The wolf must have followed your scent. You wonder if it will leave or stay and what has happened to Hannah.

Just then, a whistle sounds and the wolf crashes off. There is another whistle, closer this time, and then the wolf comes racing back to sniff at your tree and then tears back off across the glen in another direction. Someone else enters the clearing, and you and Ted look at each other trying to work out if you should call out or not. Hannah's voice interrupts your silent debate:

"Well, is anyone going to invite me into the tree?"

Ted lowers down his hand, and Hannah, ignoring it, climbs up like a monkey. You think of all those ladders in the library and wonder if that is how she got to be such a climber.

"Right," she says, very business-like. "Looks like we've got ourselves a typical enchanted forest situation. A few ways in, but as yet, no discernible way out. A flytrap of sorts. There's a big doggie out there with sharp teeth, but he likes to play fetch. Not really a problem." She looks at Ted. "You been here long?"

Ted tells Hannah his story. Blushing, he tells her that there were some beautiful girls he'd seen heading off each night, as if to a ball, and he'd wanted to dance with one of them. He'd followed them the first night and had seen them enter the ballroom and start dancing. Before long, they had disappeared from sight, and he'd felt sure if he knew the steps, he could dance his way into the heart of the last dancer.

"Hmmm," says Hannah. "So you weren't meant to land

in this trap — you've just come in the back door. I was hoping we wouldn't have to go talk to the satyrs, but we may need to find out how to get back to the house from them. They aren't always friendly. Still, we might have something we can trade."

The drumming of hooves can be heard in the distance — you look down below in time to see the wolf, who had been curled up at the foot of the tree, prick his ears and listen intently. He wags his tail and retreats into denser forest a short distance away. You can see him crouching. It isn't long before three brown pigs appear. They have long tusks and are covered in shaggy hair. They begin to root about under the peach tree. One of them runs at the tree and bangs it with his head. A few ripe peaches fall to the floor, and the pigs begin to snarl and fight over them. While they are battling for the peaches, the wolf leaps out and rushes toward them. The pigs race off, and the wolf gives chase.

"I think we should join the party," says Hannah. She climbs down from the tree and starts walking. Ted follows, and you climb cautiously down too. As you walk, you ask Ted if he's spoken to the satyrs before.

"Oh yes. After I was lost here, I asked them if they knew the way for me to get back home, but they answered me in riddles and taunted me. The librarian is right, they aren't very nice. The pigs are their pets, and they aren't very nice either. "

You head on through the trees, which seem to go on forever. This world had seemed so small from above on the tiled floor of the ballroom, but it is so much bigger here. The librarian produces another round of chocolate from her basket, and Ted's eyes light up.

"Have you got a lot of food in that basket?" he asks.

"I've got one or two goodies."

She smiles at Ted, but you think she isn't quite as confident as she was at first. The terrain around you is changing. The trees are thinning out and the seasonal changes that could be seen from a short distance — ice and snow in patches among summer greens are less evident. The wood gives way to scrub, and then the dirt starts to kick up dryly as you tread. It is desolate.

"If I had to guess, I'd say someone doesn't want us to come this way," says Hannah.

"I haven't seen this part of the woods before," says Ted.

He sounds uncertain. You wish you could do something to help. You put your hands in your pockets and check to see if there's anything useful. There's the hole — but you can't imagine that would be useful right now. And what's this? You pull out the tube you'd seen earlier today in the storeroom.

"What's that?" asks Hannah.

You hand her the tube marked 'hope', and she smiles broadly.

"I'd say this is very handy."

She breaks off the end, and you see that the tube contains doughnut-shaped lozenges. Hannah hands them around and pops one in her mouth. Ted, as always, is eager for any 'real' food.

You put the hope into your mouth and feel a rush of zingy citrus. "Lemon!" you say just as Ted calls out "Strawberry!"

"Mine is raspberry," says Hannah. "Hope must taste differently to different people. Huh? Did anyone see that building there before?"

Not too far away, a wooden building stands on its own. It has large windows at the front and a double width door. Above the door is a sign which clearly states 'Library'.

"Well, that's just dandy," exclaims Hannah. "Now we just need to enquire about returns."

She sets off again, and you and Ted follow, looking at one another and laughing. You can't believe things seemed so grim before. You head towards the building. As you do, the ground changes, becoming a little flatter and with a tile here and there, a wooden one. Around the building, the ground is different, and it starts to change underfoot as you near it. Before long, the floor resembles that of the ballroom floor earlier this morning, except instead of seeing a forest floor and satyrs and wolves and trees, you see some of the people who live in the Magician's house and even the Magician himself standing with his hands on his hips looking up at you.

Just as you are about to get to the library, there is the sound of angry squealing in the distance, and the pigs race up in a cloud of dust. The satyrs are close behind, and they laugh at you menacingly. The pigs start to blow at the library, and the building begins to buckle and sway. You pick up speed to try and get to it before it disappears. Hannah lets out a whistle, and the wolf appears and starts snarling and snapping at the pigs. They stop blowing as the wolf harasses them. The library is within reach. Ted opens the door and holds out his hand to you and tosses you inside. Then he reaches for Hannah, who is still encouraging the wolf. The satyrs have begun to angrily kick at the wolf, which dodges them as it continues to keep the pigs from destroying the library.

At last, Ted grabs on to Hannah and pulls her into the library. He is about to slam the door when Hannah grabs it and lets out a low whistle. The wolf leaps inside too as she slams the door on the angry pigs and satyrs outside. The library begins to move as if it has been picked up by a tornado. Books explode from shelves and whirl around. The wolf leans into Hannah and whines in fear. Ted steadies Hannah, but she doesn't seem to need any help that you can see. At last, the wind dies down. Hannah opens the door with the wolf beside her. She steps out, and you see you are entering the Magician's library.

Across the room, you see the door Hannah propped open earlier and beyond that … a great big hole in the ballroom floor. The Magician is standing next to it as though he is preparing to cast a spell. He waves and doesn't seem too concerned about the mess.

You are the last person to step out of the strange library. The building melts back into the library wall, leaving a door that is framed with intricate carvings of leaves and vines and little pigs and satyrs.

Congratulations, you've reached the end of this part of your story.

What would you like to do now? Do you:

Go back to the beginning of this story and try a different path? **P1**

Or

Check the list of choices and start reading from somewhere else? **P84**

You have decided to go with Charlie to get his things

It is still pretty early in the morning. Along the road, deliveries are being made in the neighborhood: bread and vegetables and meat and coal. As you round the corner of your street, Charlie exclaims and says "But that's the house we were cleaning over there. How did I end up in your master's roof? How very strange!"

If Charlie is going to be living at the Magician's house, he'll learn pretty quickly that 'strange' is an everyday event — but he's had a frightening time lately and you don't want him scared. Instead, you ask him about his family. Charlie chats about growing up outside of London in the country, the school he went to and the books he read. He might like the Magician's schoolroom — people turn up and teach and the lessons have a way of coming in handy later on, but each time you stumble upon the schoolroom it seems entirely accidental.

As you talk, the streets narrow and get busier. Charlie points at a large stone building.

"That's where my family are."

A sign outside reads *King's Bench*.

"Do you think the Magician would let me take them some scraps sometimes? They have poor food there. It's a bleak house."

You nod. Mrs. Noogles often gives away food to people who come around the back. No doubt she will find some food for Charlie's family. It does strike you as odd that

someone should be imprisoned for not paying their debts —
how would they ever get out? How could they work? Charlie
explains that often relations pool together to pay debts. He
is hopeful a family cousin will help them.

Down a small alleyway, you come to the house of the
bailiff who has taken in the sons of the debtors. It is part a
string of rickety houses built into the side of the prison's
brick wall — the only straight part of the buildings.

The bailiff's house is four rickety stories high, and
patched up here and there like a quilt with spare boards.
Like the rest of the street, there is an air of dilapidation and
squalor. You follow Charlie through a faded red door.
Inside, the building smells of boiled cabbage and sweaty
socks.

"The first floor is the bailiff's rooms," says Charlie.

As he starts up the stairs, a woman with a baby steps into
the hallway and waves to him. "Home early, Charlie?
Everything all right?"

"Yes, Mrs. Winch — everything's roses! I've found a
man's going to put me up and give me a job and he has a
schoolroom! I'm going back to school! I'm just getting my
things."

Mrs. Winch reminds him about the rent that is due and
Charlie says he will be back to pay the balance. He springs
up the stairs, beckoning you to follow. The next floor is
rented out by the room to families and couples and smells of
double cabbage and socks. You wonder what the next floor
will smell like as you start up the next set of stairs. Unlike

the Magician's house, you don't have to be careful of slipping into dreams, but there is a real danger of slipping through the floorboards as they are buckling and broken and patched.

The last floor is a converted attic. You needn't have worried about the smell because the draft carries it all away. It's cold and grim.

Charlie moves to a small pile of rags and boxes in the corner, and gathers his few things. You see his treasures are books and papers and his coat and hat. Here and there in the attic are other piles of belongings that must correspond to other boys. Charlie explains they are all children of debtors and the bailiff's family is very good to keep them. They are able to pay a small rent and also make some payment toward their family's debt. Suddenly, Charlie looks stricken.

"Do you think the Magician will pay me?"

Charlie glances around the attic, and you know he is thinking that if he can't be paid he really should stay in the grim position he was just happily leaving. You reassure him that the Magician is a strange fellow but also a fair one, and if he needs money you are sure it will be provided, especially if Charlie is helping at the theatre, because this is how the Magician earns his living. Charlie grins and looks very happy.

At the bottom of the stairs, the bailiff's wife is waiting with a baby on her hip. She puts a finger up to her lips to tell you to keep quiet. She points to her front room and then retreats to the back of the house. At her warning, you both slow down and hear gruff voices.

"You owe me a boy! That latest one didn't show this morning. I heard he was doing chimneys. I pay you good money to find me kids for the factory. Pay me back or give me another boy!"

Charlie's eyes go wide — there's obviously some arrangement about his job at the blacking factory. You both try to make your way cautiously outside to the street. Just as you are at the front door there is a banging at it. You and Charlie scarper back up the stairs and crouch down to listen from the second floor. Charlie whispers that when the coast is clear you should both run out.

Heavy steps are heard in the front passage and someone opens the front door. Peering round the banister, you see the back of a big man with a heavy belt filling the doorway. A set of large keys hangs off his wide belt. This must be Mr. Winch, the bailiff. He is talking to another man who sounds just as angry as the one in the front parlor. It is the chimney sweep, and he is complaining that he lost the new sweep straight off and he wants some money back.

The bailiff isn't quite so kind after all. He is organizing children of debtors to be used as factory workers and chimney sweeps. He is taking money from the other men and he is getting rent from the children.

"Now see here!" he tells the chimney sweep. "It's not my problem if you lose your workers down chimneys — you got to train them proper! I might find you another boy for the same arrangement, but I don't owe you nothing!"

"You owe me something, though, Winch." It is the man from the factory.

"You guaranteed me that boy for nine months of gluing. Assured me, you did! Then he's hopped off to the sweep, and he's lost him! You lost me my worker and he was a good one too — he could read! He never glued the labels upside down!"

The three men continue to argue. You feel a squeeze from Charlie. He signals you to follow him down the hall, holding his fingers to his lips to say to keep quiet.

Singing in a room off the hallway draws your attention to a doorway. Perhaps it would be a good idea to ask one of the people living on this floor to shelter you for a while? On the other hand, you and Charlie have done nothing wrong. The bailiff might be making money from other people's misfortune, but he has made his own trouble, he really doesn't own you. Maybe you should both just head through their argument and step out the front door?

It is time to make a decision. Do you:

Ask the singer if you can shelter with them? **P66**

Or

Try and run out of the house? **P81**

Ask the singer if you can shelter with them

You decide to wait it out until the men have gone from downstairs. Charlie knocks gently on the door next to you in the hallway. The singing stops and a woman's voice can be heard asking who is there. Charlie opens the door and steps inside with you following closely. If the person inside gives you up, you will be trapped.

The room inside faces the sun. The brightness momentarily blinds you after the dark dinginess of the rest of the house. You also notice with relief that you have left the smell of cabbage and dampness that overpowers the rest of the house. Instead, the air is filled with a very pleasant mix of flowers and perfumes. In the middle of the room a worktable holds all sorts of jars and bottles. Closer to the window there are potted leafy plants with pink and white and purple flowers. This is more like a room you might find in the Magician's house, not a poor London tenement building.

"What do you two want?" The voice is frail and delicate like lace and has a French accent. In amongst the clutter of bottles and beakers, you finally locate the room's occupant. She is an old woman with a grey smock over her voluminous skirts. She is carefully pouring liquid from a large container into several small bottles.

"Pardon, Madame, je suis Charles."

Charlie introduces himself in French and then asks if you can both shelter for a short while. Surely, he must be the only French speaking chimney sweep in London! The little old woman is impressed too. She asks him questions and then, realizing you are not following the conversation, politely continues in English.

She laughs wryly when she hears that Charlie's labor has been sold to both the blacking factory and the sweep.

"That rogue! You were right to be careful, Charlie. He won't want you knowing what he's up to. He may lose his job at the prison if it's known he is profiteering. You must wait here until it is safe to leave."

Just then, you hear heavy footsteps out in the corridor as the three men head up to the attic. There is a splintering sound and loud cursing as it seems one of them has met with a rotten step. You wonder if the bailiff will realize that Charlie's things are gone. You don't have to wonder for long – his voice belts out to his wife through the house.

"Myra! You seen that Charlie today? His things ain't here!"

Mrs. Winch yells back that the boy came earlier with another kid to fetch his things — she says she reminded him about the rent. The bailiff's footsteps come back down He is telling the sweep and the blacking factory manager not to worry, now there's two kids, one for each of them … as soon as he finds them.

"I'll let that Charlie know there'll be trouble for his family if he doesn't get back to work. That'll fix him. The other one's probably a stray you can put down your chimneys and nobody will miss them."

Footsteps on the landing seem to be coming closer. There is a knock on the door and the door knob begins to turn.

You shudder to think of going down a small dark chimney and look pleadingly at your host, hoping she will not give you away. She looks very angry at what she is hearing and beckons you both to step inside a wardrobe in one corner of her room by her bed. Would that be a good place to hide?

Quick! Make a decision! Where are you and Charlie going to hide? Do you:

Hide in the wardrobe? **P76**

Or

Dive under the bed? **P69**

You have decided to dive under the bed

The bailiff's feet appear on the floor just inches from you. He asks your host if she has seen two kids.

"No, monsieur."

"Well, you won't mind me having a little look around then, will you?"

His feet return to the bed, and in seconds he has grabbed both you and Charlie and is dragging you out. He hauls you both down the stairs and triumphantly presents you to the sweep and the factory manager.

"There you go, one for each of you. You'll have to lock 'em up when you aren't using them. This one knows it's a longer lag for his dad if he don't work, and no doubt this one can be convinced to do their duty too. A bit of hunger will work wonders."

The sweep looks at you with disgust. "This one doesn't seem small enough for chimneys, but since Charlie managed to wiggle out before, I'll take him again."

The blacking factory owner grabs you by the back of your shirt. "This one doesn't seem to cough. I lose them to the black lung after six months of stirring the pots. Give me a rope."

While the bailiff goes for a rope, you struggle to get free of the factory manager's arms. Meanwhile, Charlie's face is twisted in anguish. He looks terrified to be going back to the dark chimneys. His predicament might be worse than your own.

You have an idea and look at the sweep. "My master sent me back here to get your name. You left your boy in his chimney, and he wants you to pay for the damage he caused."

The sweep looks cautious. "Now steady on here — a boy getting stuck isn't my fault."

The greedy factory manager recognizes an opportunity and turns to the sweep. "Tell you what, since you can't have him running around ruining your good name, how about you give that one to me as well and I'll keep him secure."

The sweep nods and starts deliberating about money with the bailiff, as he feels he has paid for something he didn't get. Mr. Winch ends up agreeing to give him some coins and then ties both of you up.

Charlie doesn't look much happier but you think if you're both together you might be able to find a way back to the Magician's house. You try to give him a reassuring look.

The blacking factory man whistles out the front door to where another man in a horse and cart is waiting. He jumps down from his seat and comes inside to help your captor. The two men toss you on the back of the cart with a rag tied over your mouth to keep you from yelling out. In this part of London, you doubt anyone would come to your aid anyway. A smelly tarpaulin is thrown over you. There is just enough light to see Charlie's frightened eyes as the cart starts moving down the lane.

You have only travelled a few streets before the cart stops once more. There are voices. Then the tarp is moved, and you are hoisted over the back of a man and taken inside a building you guess must be the blacking factory. You are taken down some stairs and dumped on a pile of sacks. Charlie lands with a woof of dust beside you. The manager addresses him:

"Well, Charlie, you've lost me a good day's work, if not more. The rest of the boys have probably been slacking off while I've been out chasing you. It's not good for business, boy. From now on, you'll be staying here with your friend, and we can take what you owe me out of your wages. I've half a mind to beat you black and blue, but that will probably just make you slower. Starting tomorrow, I want you two working. Tonight, you'll sleep down here with the rats — that will give you a taste of what it's like to cross me. It's just a taste, mind. You don't want to go doing that regular."

He picks up a stick and tosses it towards you both.

"This should give you a fighting chance against being bitten. With any luck, you'll clear a few rats out for me."

With that, he loosens the ropes around Charlie's arms, and heads back up the cellar stairs. You hear a deadbolt slide home on the other side of the door. There is faint light coming from under the door and a little more shows between the floorboards over your head. You hear Charlie moving around getting untied. He isn't the only one rustling. Rats are coming out of the corners to see what might be worth picking over.

Once Charlie has freed himself, he helps you too. The

two of you stand up, rubbing the places where the ropes had rubbed at your wrists, and look at your prison.

"I've lost my books," says Charlie, and a few tears start to leak from his grimy face.

You look at him and laugh. "Charlie, we're locked in a cellar with the light fading and a horde of rats about to bite us, and *you* are crying about books."

Charlie smiles and awkwardly wipes the tears away. He starts apologizing to you for the trouble you are in. You hush him quiet and are about to tell him not to worry when a rat makes a dash across Charlie's boot and bites at his shoe lace. He shoos the rat away by stamping and picks up the stick.

"I have an idea about the rats," you say. "Did you happen to put anything from breakfast in your pocket?"

Shamefacedly, Charlie nods. From his trouser pocket, he pulls a rather mangled piece of toast, and from your own pocket you pull out the hole you folded up and tucked away this morning. Charlie watches, astonished, as you lay it out on the floor like a carpet. As soon as the hole is laid down the ladder appears — inviting you in.

"Are we going down there?" asks Charlie.

"I'm not sure," you say, "but hopefully the rats are."

You sprinkle a line of crumbs close to the hole and carefully sprinkle some more down the sides. You both stand back to watch.

Before long, the boldest rats are scampering toward the hole and munching on the crumbs. Others follow not wanting to miss out. Thinking there is a feast inside, they swarm down the sides — you count at least fifty. You hope the creature inside enjoys them as much as mice.

Now that the rat problem is over, you look around the cellar to see if there is any way out. It's built of stone blocks, and the walls are very solid. You walk to the back behind barrels of foul-smelling stuff and more piles of sacks, but find the cellar has no other way out.

Charlie has been searching too. He comes down the cellar stairs from where he has been checking the door and peers into the hole. "Where does that go?"

"I don't know." You explain that you think there will be an opening down the ladder, but you have no idea where.

Charlie asks if he has heard correctly and that when you first explored the hole its bottom was on the ceiling. You nod. Charlie looks around and finds half a brick. He leans over the hole and drops it in. You both listen. Splash! Wherever the hole ends up, it's a wet ending. Then you hear a yell, and Charlie says he thinks it's a boy who works stirring the blacking pot upstairs. The hole might come out right over the boiling cauldron. You certainly don't want to end up in that.

A big cat face emerges from the hole. "Thanks for the rats, my friend, but luckily I missed the brick." It looks around. "This isn't the Magician's house is it?"

"Sorry about the brick," Charlie stammers, "We are attempting to escape from this cellar and I was trying to determine where the hole would lead us."

The black cat eyes him and evidently decides to forgive him for chucking the brick down its hole. "Then I suggest the hole be repositioned somewhere which would allow you both an alternative exit."

After the cat disappears, you pick up the portable hole and think about where it might be best to put it next.

Charlie, though, is way ahead of you. "If we put it on the floor and it comes out in the ceiling of the room above, it might follow that if we put it against the far wall we might get out of the front door!"

He's really quite clever and completely wasted putting labels on jars, you think. The two of you take hold of the hole and then cast it like a fishing net at the back wall of the cellar, hoping it will form a tunnel rather than a hole.

It works.

When it lands this time, there is no ladder, and you can just walk inside. Near the entrance of the hole, there are glowworms to light the path, but just as before they soon give way to darkness. You are out in front and, before long, your foot finds the end of the path and a custardy nothing beyond it.

"Jump, kittens!" You hear the cat say. So taking each other's hands you both leap. The two of you fall in slow motion. Eventually, you land on a heap of sacks by the front door of the factory beside a black tunnel that looks like it was blasted into the brick wall of the factory.

Quickly, you roll up the hole and stuff it back in your pocket. In moments, you are both running towards the

Magician's house and clapping each other on the back, congratulating each other on your escape.

Congratulations, you've reached the end of this part of your story.

What would you like to do now? Do you:

Go back to the beginning of this story? **P1**

Or

Check the list of choices to read from somewhere else? **P84**

You have decided to hide in the wardrobe

Just as the wardrobe door shuts, the bailiff enters the room.

Through the keyhole, you see a barrel-chested man with long greasy hair tied up at his neck. A leather belt stretches around his waist from which jangles a bundle of large keys. He asks the French lady if she has seen two runaway kids.

"Their parents are debtors."

She says she hasn't seen you, but he strides into the room and looks around anyway. She asks him to leave, saying he will damage her things, but he ignores her. He crouches low and looks under the bed you nearly hid under. He takes another look around and then leaves. The lady puts her fingers to her lips and gestures for you to stay put. Next to you, Charlie is fidgeting.

"Is he gone?" he whispers.

"Shhhh," you hiss.

The bailiff heads back downstairs. You listen to muffled talking from the three men. Then there is one, then two, and a short while later, a third bang of the front door. All this time the lady has been patiently working with her bottles. When the last man leaves, she gets up and beckons you both out of the wardrobe. You both thank her for hiding you. Your rescuer introduces herself as Mignette.

"I'm happy to have helped, children. I know what it's like to be hunted. I escaped from Paris during the revolution. You never knew if you would be next to be imprisoned or worse. So I packed what I could of my business and came by boat to London."

"What is your business, Madame Mignette?" you ask.

"Why, perfume, of course! All the rich ladies need perfume so they do not have to smell the filth of the streets and to make the men think they are like flowers themselves!"

Mignette points to the row of little bottles she is filling and offers you a sniff. The delicate scent of flowers wafts from each small vial. You watch Mignette place a small cork stopper in each and then melt wax around the cork to keep it secure. Lastly, she reaches for glue and labels, but Charlie stops her:

"I know the drill, madame," he declares and deftly adds a label to each perfume bottle while Mignette goes on to fill another batch. Having watched the process, you help with the corks and wax and the three of you complete her work.

After a while Mignette suggests you are both probably safe to leave. "If they were watching the building, they have probably gone." She hands you both a small bottle of perfume as thanks for the morning's work. You thank her again and warily head out of her apartment.

Outside, you keep a sharp eye out as you head back to the Magician's house. Before long, you are entering the servants' entrance and looking at the disapproving face of Mrs. Noogles. You have been away all morning and haven't been any help in the kitchen. Lunch looks to be almost prepared. Charlie hands her his bottle of perfume and says you both stopped to earn a gift for her. Mrs. Noogles breaks into a grin and tells you that you deserved some time off.

"Now get your young selves off to the schoolroom, and I'll see you when it's time to eat again."

With a sinking feeling, you realize you haven't done your homework. Maybe a new pupil will distract Miss Spurlock. You glance at Charlie and see he is giddy with excitement at the prospect of schooling. You have to smile — school can be a chore but you know it would beat working in the blacking factory or cleaning chimneys any day. You show him to the door that you hope will lead you to the schoolroom. As you head down the corridor, you resume your careful walking and explain to Charlie that this house has its own equivalent of faulty floorboards. Charlie is disbelieving until you both wander into a patch of carpet that acts like sand and causes you to drag your feet and hear gulls in the distance. You take his hand and guide him to the wall where your footing is surer, and before long you are entering the schoolroom.

Miss Spurlock looks up from a book she is reading the class as you both enter the classroom. She smiles at Charlie and says she has been expecting a new student today. She asks Charlie about his education, and he chatters about books he has read.

"You like stories, Charlie?"

"Very much, Miss."

Miss Spurlock says she'd like him to write her a story so she can get an idea of his education so far. She hands him paper and ink. Then she hands you a list of mathematical problems to practice.

The thing about Miss Spurlock is she always comes up with fascinating math problems. The first one is about calculating how many cream cakes you would have to eat if you were trapped in a pile of them and the way out was a trap door in the floor. Her instructions always say *show your workings.* Miss Spurlock says the workings are more important than the answer when you are learning to reckon. You know there may not be a perfect answer, but it is fun to consider. You sit down and think about what you know, and soon your mind is deep in numbers and their logic. Charlie scrawls furiously beside you. When Miss Spurlock sends you out to help with lunch, he is still scribbling.

Back in the kitchen with Mrs. Noogles, you set out the dinner plates, and she again tells you the Magician will join you all for the meal. You are slicing tomatoes for the salad when everyone else arrives to eat. Miss Spurlock is looking very happy. When the Magician arrives, she suggests to him that Charlie reads his story to everybody. The gardeners look a little uncomfortable at this, and you can tell they think the story will be boring and might interfere with the Victoria sponge cake Mrs. Noogles has ready for dessert.

Charlie looks nervous, but the Magician says it is a magnificent idea and he would love to hear it. So Charlie stands up and begins his tale.

You can't believe it! He has taken your adventures this morning and dressed them up. He describes Mignette and her escape from France with so much more detail. The maids and gardeners gasp and worry if she will make it to safety. Charlie stops just as all seems to be lost:

"Should I keep reading, or am I keeping us from cake?" he asks with the knowing smile of a born performer.

"Keep reading! Keep reading!" everyone cries.

Then Charlie describes fisticuffs between the bailiff and the chimney sweep and finally the hero — Charlie Dickens — is saved with his friend (you!) and is able to attend a fine classroom and eat first-rate food. Everybody cheers at the end and Miss Spurlock tells him he has a talent for telling stories.

"You should keep it up."

Congratulations, you've reached the end of this part of your story.

What would you like to do now? Do you:

Go back to the beginning of this story? **P1**

Or

Check the list of choices to read from somewhere else? **P84**

You have decided to try and run out of the house

Halfway down the stairs, Mr. Winch steps out above you and the factory manager steps out below.

You both try to get to the door but it's useless, and the two men overpower you and truss you up like a chicken for the roasting pan. You are gagged and put into big sacks and thrown on the back of a cart. In no time, you are carried into the blacking factory where Charlie worked before he became a chimney sweep.

The factory manager throws you both into a room with jars and labels and says just three words:

"Get to work!"

He closes the door, and you hear a bolt being slid on the other side, locking you in.

"I'm so sorry," says Charlie. A tear escapes down his cheek.

"Don't worry," you say.

You've remembered the hole in your pocket. Charlie watches as you place it on the floor. The ladder appears and Charlie follows you down.

"Where does this go?" asks Charlie. You have to tell him you don't know, but it seems like a good way to get out of the factory. After a while, you hear the voice of the factory manager above. He's discovered the hole, and it sounds as if he's following you down.

"Jump," you tell Charlie. You pull him loose from the ladder. Your fall is slow, like moving through custard. When you land you recognize the foot of the grand stairs — you are back in the Magician's house.

"Step exactly where I step," you tell Charlie and head up the stairs. About half way up, there is a bit of a trap for the unwary traveler. If you head up the middle, you'll end up in the middle of a party, crowded with people. You know how to avoid it, though, by skipping up the side. Charlie follows, and you are nearly at the top of the stairs when the factory manager comes out of the hole. He is only slightly surprised to find himself in a grand house and immediately leaps up the stairs to catch you both.

Charlie moves as if to run, but you tell him to wait. As you expected, the manager disappears into a crowd of people. He's now trapped in the party. You and Charlie slide down the banister and nearly bump into the Magician.

"Have you been bringing vermin into the house?" he asks you.

"Sorry sir, we had to, we were being chased," says Charlie.

The factory manager has just made it out of the party. He looks very confused but still very, very angry.

"Don't worry, lad," says the Magician, and he snaps his fingers. The factory manager turns into a fat black rat. The rat sees your hole in the ground and runs down it.

A few seconds later, there is a squeak and a purring voice from the hole speaks up, "Delicious!"

"Right, you two, off to the schoolroom," says the Magician.

Congratulations, you've reached the end of this part of your story.

What would you like to do now? Do you:

Go back to the beginning of this story and try a different path? **P1**

Or

Check the list of choices and pick some other part of the story to read? **P84**

List of Choices

Bonus Story and Previews

BONUS STORY

Christmas in the Magician's House

(First published in *The Best of Twisty Christmas Tales*, Phantom Feather Press, 2014.)

Ever since I fell down its chimney, I've lived in the Magician's house. I could leave, but I don't want to. Working for the Magician is much better than being a chimney sweep.

They like me here too. Mrs. Noogles, the cook, says I'm one of the best people she knows at finding my way around. She gave me a red frog on the morning I arrived. Well, she didn't exactly give it to me, what she said was, "Get that frog out of my way, or it's going to end up in the rhubarb pie."

Perched on a rhubarb leaf was a frog the same color as the ruby stalks. I'd never seen a red frog before.

"Come on," I said. And like a pet dog, it's been following me around ever since.

It's a strange house, this one. Rooms don't stay in the same place. Stairs take you back in time — which is good if you want two breakfasts — but sometimes doors just disappear. You can't even expect to find the same room behind a door twice. Things change all the time. I can cope with that, but I'm worried about Christmas. I don't have a present for the Magician or Mrs. Noogles, and we're meant to be exchanging presents tonight.

The house has dressed itself up. The suit of armor is wearing a velvet sash, and turns up all over the place, even though I never see it move. The walls are covered with tapestries. My favorite has a forest embroidered on it. Yesterday, when I stopped to look at it, I noticed sparkly little decorations stitched onto every tree.

I missed last Christmas. I came across a jiggling basket with a lid. Of course, I wondered what could be inside. Would it do any harm to look? Next thing I knew, a snake popped out and sank its fangs into my arm. It felt like being stabbed by two icicles.

I didn't even make it to the door before I turned to stone. Later, the gardeners came in and tipped me into a wheel-barrow. They took me outside and stuck me in the back garden, where for months I watched my red frog jumping around in the rhubarb and worried it might get stuck in a pie. When a lightning storm finally unfroze me, it was way past Christmas. If I don't find presents soon, I might need to open that basket again.

The Magician is pretty busy this time of year. He's got a special theatre where he works. There's a big curtain along one wall. When we raise the curtain, the audience could be in London or Paris or New York — you never know where you'll be when you open a door to the outside.

Last time I left the garden, I found myself on a beach. It wasn't cold like London, with grimy roof tops — instead there were warm blue skies, and trees with feathery red flowers. When I asked about it later, Mrs. Noogles told me I'd been to New Zealand.

"The house likes it there," she said.

Thinking about presents, and following the scent of Mrs. Noogles' muffin, I got distracted. The smell of spice and rhubarb was so good that when I opened the door to where the kitchen was yesterday, I stepped through without looking and ended up in the library.

There was a plate of food, all right, next to a pile of books on the table. The door vanished. Now all the walls were lined with bookcases. The Magician's house had tricked me again.

Sitting down at the table, I reached for a rhubarb muffin — no sense starving to death while I waited for something to happen. As I bit into a muffin, the red frog croaked. There it was, under the table, sitting on the floor beside a fishing net.

"Hello, little fellow," I said. I would have given it a muffin, but that's not the sort of thing it eats. It's a pretty big frog now — about the size of a kitten. It jumped onto the table by the books, as if it wanted to hear a story.

The top book was covered in rich, blue leather; its title was in a language I didn't know. I nibbled my muffin. I told you about what happened with the snake in a basket — well, you can't always trust the books around here either. Surely, there wasn't a snake inside it, though.

I opened the book. The writing inside swirled about and a

picture started to form- I could see a mountain. And smell a mountain and feel the air change around me. It was more like opening a window than a book. The library became very cold. A bird flew out of the picture, grabbed what was left of the muffin out of my hand, and flew back in again. When a flock of birds started to fly towards me, I quickly flipped the page, and soon the room warmed up again.

When I came to a picture that looked into a shop, I stopped. It was a strange shop with all sorts of curiosities lining the shelves. A snow globe caught my eye — you know the sort of thing, you shake it and it snows on the scene inside. This one held a tiny house, just like the Magician's house. I wanted to touch it, but it was just out of my reach. I brought the net out from under the table and was about to try again when the shop door opened, and two ruffians walked in. I know bullies when I see them. I met a few when I was cleaning chimneys.

As they swaggered towards the counter, a shopkeeper came out to meet them.

"Have you got the money?" asked one of the bullies.

The shopkeeper shook his head nervously. The bigger bully leant over the counter and growled.

"How are we going to keep your shop safe if you don't pay?" But the shopkeeper wasn't going to be intimidated. He stood up straight and shook his head again.

The other bully pulled a cage out from under his coat and opened it.

The shopkeeper turned pale as a swarm of green insects

flew out. They started to bang into the things on the shelves. A yellow vase crashed to the floor. The bullies ran out of the shop, laughing, as the shopkeeper leapt around trying to catch the things the insects were knocking off the shelves.

The red frog's tongue snapped through the page, and caught one of the green bugs. Then it jumped through the book into the shop. Still holding the net I sprang through the picture after it and joined the red frog catching the destructive little beasts. The frog bounded about, snapping with its tongue. Those bugs knew we were after them. Two of them started to beat themselves against the window, clattering against the delicate glass. I was worried they would break it, but the frog's tongue shot out and made short work of them. When we'd caught them all, the shopkeeper fetched a jar for the creatures in my net. He put a few leaves in the jar. Whatever the leaves were, they calmed those things right down.

"Thank you so much," he said. "I thought I was going to lose all my treasures. Please choose something from the shelves as a thank you."

What a stroke of luck! I picked the snow globe for Mrs. Noogles.

When I turned to go back to the library, I couldn't see the way.

The shopkeeper smiled and held up a blue leather book. "I think this will help."

Flicking through the book's pages cautiously, afraid of what might fly out, I came to a picture of the Magician's library. The frog and I stepped through and, to my surprise, just before I closed the book again, the shopkeeper handed me the jar of insects.

Back in the Magician's house, the library door had reappeared, so I headed through before it could disappear again. Just in time – all the staff were exchanging presents.

I handed Mrs. Noogles her snow globe – she looked really pleased. Then I turned to the Magician, about to say I was sorry I didn't have a present for him when I saw the big smile through his beard. He took the jar of annoying insects, bashing themselves against the thick glass walls.

"Pandemonium dragon flies!" he said. "Just the thing for my terrarium."

The jar burst...

"Merry Christmas," I said.

Previews of More
'You Say Which Way' Adventures

Preview: The Creepy House

Shhh! What's that noise?

Your family got a cheap deal on a bigger house, and the day you move in you find out why. Right next-door is a creepy old place that looks like the set for a horror movie. Your family says it has character but you think it might have rats … or worse.

Your cat is locked in the spare room while the movers are going in and out so she doesn't get lost. The cat was a bribe from your family to accept moving across town away from all your friends. She's small and gray and came from the animal shelter. You've thought of the perfect name for her: Ghost.

After the movers have gone and the doors are shut downstairs, you let Ghost out to explore her new home. She comes into your room as you're putting away the last of your books and jumps on your bed.

"Hello Ghost. Do you like your new home?"

You settle down next to her with your book. It's called *Between the Stars* and it's about a weird space ship of sleeping travelers who wake up for adventures. It's really good but you're gradually distracted by a tapping at the window.

That's odd, it's a second story window.

There's a tall tree just outside, it must be making the noise. You open the window and see that a branch is caught on some old wires. You untangle the wires just as you hear "Dinner's ready!" from downstairs. Your stomach growls, you don't need telling twice.

When you come back, Ghost isn't on your bed anymore and you can feel a breeze from the open window. As you start to shut it, you see your cat disappearing inside a window next door. She has climbed through the tree over to that spooky house.

"Ghost! Ghost! Puss, puss, puss!"

Through tattered drapes, you can make out an old-fashioned bed over there. A movement in the opposite room catches your eye and then you recognize yourself reflected in a long grimy mirror. You shiver. There's no sign of Ghost.

It is time to make your first decision. Do you:

Go over to the house and try to get your cat back?

Or

Leave the window open and wait for her to return?

Preview: The Sorcerer's Maze - Jungle Trek

One moment you were at home reading a book and now you're standing in the jungle, deep in the Amazon rainforest.

Beside you flows a slow-moving river, murky brown from all the silt it carries downstream. Monkeys screech in the tall trees across the water. The air is hot and buzzing with insects. As you watch, the tiny flying creatures gather together in an unnatural cloud formation and then separate to form words:

WELCOME they spell in giant letters.

This is crazy you think.

NOPE, IT'S NOT CRAZY spell the insects. THIS IS THE START OF THE SORCERER'S MAZE.

The insect cloud bursts apart and the tiny creatures buzz off. What's next, you wonder?

Twenty yards away two kids, about your age, stand beside a small boat with a small outboard motor attached to its stern. The boat has a blue roof to protect its occupants from the hot tropical sun.

They both smile and wave.

The girl walks towards you. "Do you want a ride up river?" she asks. "My brother and I know the Amazon well."

"Do you work for the sorcerer?" you ask. "He designed the maze, didn't he?"

The girl nods. "Yes. My brother and I are his apprentices. The sorcerer wants you to have company while you're here."

The two of you walk back down to the river's edge.

"This is Rodrigo. I'm Maria."

You drop your daypack into the dugout and hold out your hand. "Hi Rodrigo, interesting looking boat."

Rodrigo shakes your hand. "It does the job. But before we can go upriver," he says, pulling a piece of paper out of his pocket. "The sorcerer wants me to ask you a question. If you get it right, we can leave."

"And if not?" you ask.

"I've got more questions," the boy says, patting his pocket. "I'm sure you'll get one right eventually." He unfolds the paper. "Okay, here's your first question. Which of the following statements is true?"

It is time to make a decision. Which do you choose?

The Amazon River has over 3000 known species of fish.

Or

The Amazon River has less that 1000 known species of fish.

Preview: Secrets of Glass Mountain

With the screech of diamonds on smooth black rock, a troop of Highland Sliders comes skidding to a stop ten yards from you and your schoolmates.

"That's what I want to do when I leave school," says Dagma. "Being a Highland Slider looks like so much fun."

Another classmate shakes his head. "Yeah, but my cousin went mining and struck it rich on his first trip out. Now he owns two hydro farms and his family live in luxury."

You look around the small settlement where you grew up. It's a beautiful place, high on the Black Slopes of Petron. Far below, past the sharp ridges and towering pinnacles, the multicolored fields of the Lowlands stretch off into the distance. At the horizon, a pink moon sits above a shimmering turquoise sea.

But the beauty isn't enough to keep you here. You could never be a farmer or a merchant. You've always dreamed of travel and adventure.

Maybe mining is the right thing to do. You imagine heading off into the wild interior looking for diamonds and the many secrets these glass mountains contain. Imagine striking it rich!

Or do you become a slider like so many others from your family? What would happen to your home without the protection of the Highland Sliders? How would people move around the dangerous slopes, from settlement to settlement, without their expert guidance? And who would stop the Lowlanders from invading?

Your part in this story is about to begin. You will leave school at the end of the week and it's time for you to choose your future.

It is time to make your first decision. Do you:

Start cadet training to become a slider?

Or

Go to mining school so you can prospect for diamonds?

Preview: Between the Stars.

In a sleep tank on the space ship *Victoria*, your dreaming cap teaches you as you float.

You first put on a dreaming cap for the space sleep test. Although you thought it looked like you had an octopus on your head, you didn't joke about it. Nobody did. Everyone wanted to pass the test and go to the stars.

Passing meant a chance to get out of overcrowded Londinium.

If you didn't pass, you'd likely be sent to a prison factory in Northern Europa. Nobody wanted to go there, even though Britannica hasn't been a good place lately, Europa was said to be worse.

When the judge sentenced you to transportation for stealing that food, you sighed inside with relief. You knew transportation was the chance of a better life on a faraway planet, but only if you passed the sleep test.

You lined up with other hopefuls and waded into a pool of warm sleep jelly. They were all young, like you, and they all looked determined.

"Stay calm," the robot instructed. "Breathe in slowly through your mouthpiece and relax."

Nearby, a young woman struggled from the pool. She pulled out her breathing plug and gasped for breath.

"Take her back," said a guard. You knew what that meant – back to prison and then the factories. A convict sneered at the poor girl, the cruel look on his face magnified by a scar running down one cheek.

In your short time in prison, you had learned there were people who would have been criminals no matter what life they'd been born to. Something told you that he was one of them.

You put him out of your mind and concentrated on doing what the robot said. You thought of the warm porridge you'd had every morning in the orphanage growing up. The sleeping jelly didn't seem so strange then. When your head was submerged, you breathed in slowly.

As the jelly filled your lungs, you fought against thoughts of drowning. You'd listened at the demonstration and knew it was oxygenated. *This must be what it's like to be a fish*, you'd thought as you moved forward through the thick fluid, *I only have to walk through to the other side.*

Closing your eyes, you moved forward through the thick warm jelly. "Relax," you told yourself. "You can do this."

You opened your eyes just in time to see the scar-faced youth about to knock your breather off. Thankfully, the jelly slowed his punch and you ducked out of the way just in time.

Then, a moment later, you were on the other side being handed a towel.

"This one's a yes," intoned a man in a white coat. He slapped a bracelet on your wrist and sent you down a corridor away from your old life. As you exited, you just had time to hear the fate of the scar-faced youth. "He'll do. Take him to the special room."

Days of training followed. You often joined other groups of third class passengers but you didn't see Scar-Face among them. You passed all the tests and then one day, you got into a sleep tank beside hundreds of others. Your dreaming cap would teach you everything you'd need to know in your new life.

You were asleep when the *Victoria* was launched into space. You slept as the *Victoria* lost sight of the Earth and then its star, the sun.

And here you are, years later, floating in sleep fluid and learning with your dreaming cap. Or you were. Because now you hear music.

Oxygen hisses into your sleeping chamber and the fluid you have been immersed in starts to drain away. Next time you surface, you'll breathe real air, something that your lungs haven't done in a long time.

"Sleeper one two seven six do you accept this mission? Sleeper, please engage if you wish to awaken for this mission. Sleeper, there are other suitable travelers for this mission. Do you choose to wake?"

Passengers can sleep the entire journey if they want. They can arrive at the new planet without getting any older. First class passengers will own land and riches when they arrive but you're third class, you have nothing. Groggily, you listen to the voice. If you choose to take on a mission, you can earn credit for the new planet – even freedom – but you could also arrive on the new planet too old to ever use your freedom.

"Sleeper, do you accept the mission?"

It is time to make your first decision.

Do you want to wake up and undertake this mission?

Or

Do you wait for a different mission or wait to land on the new planet?

Preview: Lost in Lion Country

You only jumped out of the Land Rover for a second to take a photo. How did the rest of your tour group not notice? You were standing right beside the vehicle taking photos of a giraffe. It's not like you walked off somewhere.

The next thing you know, dust is flying and you're breathing exhaust fumes as the Land Rover races off after the pride of lions your group has been following all morning.

'Wait for me!' you scream as loud as you can. 'Wait for me!'

Unfortunately, the sound of the revving diesel engine drowns out your cries. Surely, one of your family members on the safari will notice you're missing. Maybe that nice teacher lady from Chicago you were chatting to earlier will wonder where you are. Won't the driver realize he's one person short?

You smack yourself on the forehead. This will teach you for sitting alone in the back row while the others on the safari sat up front to hear the driver's commentary.

'This is not good,' you say to yourself.

What are you going to do now? It's just as well you packed a few emergency supplies in your daypack before you boarded the tour. You have bottled water, a couple of sandwiches, a chocolate bar, your pocketknife and your trusty camera. But these things won't help you if you're seen by hungry lions, leopards, cheetah or one of the other predators that stalk the savannah.

With the vehicle now only a puff of dust in the distance, you notice something else much closer, a pack of hyenas. These scavengers weren't a problem when you were in the vehicle, but now you're on foot and the hyenas are heading your way!

You know from all the books on African wildlife you've read, these dog-like animals can be vicious and have been known to work as a team to bring down much larger animals. They would have no problem making short work of you if they wanted to.

If they find you out here all alone in the Serengeti National Park, you will be in big trouble.

You look around. What should you do? You know that normally the thing to do when you get lost is to stay put so others can find you when they come looking, but the hyenas make that impossible.

Off to your right is a large acacia tree that you might be able to climb, while on your left is a dried up creek bed.

With the hyenas getting closer, you have to move.

You decide to run over and climb up the large acacia tree

The giraffe has moved off to look for more tasty leaves. As you head towards the acacia tree, you keep looking over your shoulder at the pack of hyenas to see if they have spotted you. Luckily, the pack is upwind so their keen noses may have not picked up your scent yet, especially with all the wildebeest and zebra in the area. Still, they are covering the ground faster than you are.

The hyenas are funny looking animals. Unlike dogs, their front legs are slightly longer than their back legs, causing them to slope up towards their head. The members of this pack have light brown bodies with black spots, black faces, and funny rounded ears. If you weren't so afraid of being eaten by them, you'd stop and take photos.

You're nearly at the tree when one of the hyenas perks up its ears and yips to the others. Suddenly the whole pack is running as fast as they can right at you!

There is no time to waste. You run as fast as you can towards the tree and start looking for a way up. Luckily, you can just reach one of the lower branches. You pull yourself up by clamping your legs around the trunk and grabbing every handhold the tree offers. Once you're up on the first limb, the climbing gets easier.

The hyenas are under the tree now, eagerly yipping to each other. A couple of scrawny looking ones take a run at the tree and jump, snapping at your legs. You pull your legs up, and climb a little higher. They circle the tree and stare up at you with their black beady eyes. You are trapped.

You take off your daypack and slip out your camera. No point in missing a great photo opportunity just because you're in a spot of danger. After taking a couple shots, you pull out your water bottle and have a sip. You don't want to drink too much because you're not sure when you'll find more. The grasses on the savannah are turning brown, so you doubt there has been much rain recently. You can see down into the creek from here and it looks bone dry.

Some of the hyenas lay down in the shade of the tree. Their tongues hang out of their mouths. Are they going to wait you out? Do they think you will fall?

You remember reading that hyenas hunt mainly at night. Are they going to hang around in the shade until sundown? How will your family find you if you have to stay up here?

You could be in for a long wait and try to make yourself comfortable. After wedging your backside in between two branches and hooking your elbow around another, you start to think about what to do to get out of this situation.

It is pretty obvious that climbing down and running for it would be a disastrous idea. The pack of hyena would have you for lunch before you could get five steps. Maybe when they realize they can't get to you, the pack will move on. Or maybe they will see something that is more likely to provide them with an easy meal.

Just as you're about to lose hope, you see a dust cloud in the distance. It is getting bigger. Is the dust cloud being caused by animals or is it the Land Rover coming back for you?

You stand up and look through the leaves and shimmering haze rising from the grassy plain. Further out on the savannah thousands of wildebeest are on the move.

Surely the cloud is moving too fast to be animals. Then you see the black and white Land Rover owned by the safari tour company. But will they see you? The track is quite some distance away from the tree you are in. You didn't realize you'd come so far.

You scold yourself for not leaving something in the road to mark your position. You yell and wave and wish you'd worn bright clothing so the others could see you through the spindly leaves, but the Land Rover isn't stopping. It drives right past your position and races off in the other direction.

'Come back!' you yell.

You sit down again and think. What can you do? It looks like you're on your own, for now at least.

Then you remember the sandwiches in your daypack. Maybe the hyenas would leave you alone if you gave them some food? But then, what happens if they don't leave and you're stuck up the tree for a long time and get hungry?

A pair of vultures land in the bleached branches of a dead tree not far away. Do they know something you don't?

It is time to make a decision. Do you:

Throw the hyenas your sandwiches and hope they will eat them and leave?

Or

Keep your food for later and prepare for a long wait?

Preview: Volcano of Fire

You sit at a long table in the command pod atop one of the twin Pillars of Haramon. The room is filled with the hum of voices. A small robotic bird, unseen by those in the room, hovers in one corner.

The man at the head of the table has three blue-diamond stars pinned to his chest, indicating his rank as chief of the council. Next to him sits a visiting Lowland general, his face as hard as the rock walls of the command pod. Around the table, other important figures from both the Highlands and the Lowlands sit nervously.

Being the newest member of the Highland Council, you have yet to earn your first star, but you have big plans to make your mark.

"Quiet please," the chief says. "We've got important matters to discuss."

The chief's scars are visible, even from your seat at the opposite end of the table. These scars are proof of the many battles and expeditions he has taken part in over his long career and are proof of the dangers of living in the Highlands where the rock under your feet is the slipperiest material imaginable. Black glass.

"Supplies of tyranium crystals have run desperately low," the chief says. "Without tyranium, workers can't move safely around the slopes and that means no progress on the trade routes being built between the Lowlands and the Highlands. If our truce is to last, trade is critical."

As the chief talks, you stare out of the large windows that overlook the slopes below. Further down Long Gully, the second pillar rises from the smooth black slope. A colony of red-beaked pangos squabble with each other for nesting spaces in the cracks near its summit.

To the south are the patchwork fields of the Lowlands, the blue ribbons of the river delta and the turquoise sea. Petron's smallest moon has just risen, pale pink in the morning light, just above the horizon.

"We need to mount an expedition to locate a new source of crystals, and soon," the chief says. "Led by someone we trust."

He turns and looks in your direction. "Someone who knows how to slide on black glass and has the ability to lead a team. Someone with a knowledge of mining and brave enough to take chances when necessary. Are you up for it?" the chief asks, catching you off guard.

"Me?" Sure, you've been a troop leader in the Slider Corps and spent some time in mining school, but leading an expedition into new territory? That's quite a responsibility.

The Lowland general stands, rests his hairy knuckles on the table before him, and leans towards your end of the table. "We need someone who is respected by both the Lowlanders and the Highlanders. Someone both sides trust to ensure an equal share of any discoveries."

"That's right," the chief says. "It was you who helped start the peace process. You are the logical choice."

Your part in this story is about to begin. You are being

asked to undertake a dangerous mission, one that is important to your community. But are you really qualified? You are young. Surely, others would be more suitable. Maybe you should suggest someone more experienced lead the expedition, then you could go back home and live a safe life growing hydro or hunting pangos.

It is time to make your first decision. Do you:

Agree to lead the mission?

Or

Suggest someone else lead the mission?

Preview: Dangers of Dolphin Island

It's obvious, from the floatplane's window, how Dolphin Island got its name. The Island is shaped like a dolphin leaping out of the water. A sparkling lagoon forms the curve of the dolphin's belly, two headlands to the east form its tail and to the west another forms the dolphin's nose. As the plane banks around, losing altitude in preparation for its lagoon landing, the island's volcanic cone resembles a dorsal fin on the dolphins back.

"Wow look at that volcano," shouts a kid in the seat in front of you. "There's steam coming from the crater."

The plane's pontoons kick up a rooster-tail of spray as they touch down on the lagoon's clear water. As the plane slows, the pilot revs the engine and motors towards a wooden wharf where a group of smiling locals await your arrival.

"Welcome to Dolphin Island," the resort staff say as they secure the plane, unload your bags, and assist you across the narrow gap to the safety of a small timber wharf.

Coconut palms fringe the lagoon's white-sand beach. Palm-thatched huts poke out of the surrounding jungle. The resort's main building is just beyond the beach opposite the wharf. Between the wharf's rustic planks, you can see brightly colored fish dart back and forth amongst the coral. You stop and gaze down at the world beneath your feet.

You hear a soft squeak behind you and step aside as a young man in cut-off shorts trundles past pushing a trolley with luggage on it. He whistles a song as he passes, heading towards the main resort building. You and your family follow.

"Welcome to Dolphin Island Resort," a young woman with a bright smile and a pink flower tucked behind her ear says from behind the counter as you enter the lobby. "Here is the key to your quarters. Enjoy your stay."

Once your family is settled into their beachfront bungalow, you're eager to explore the island. You pack a flashlight, compass, water bottle, pocketknife, matches, mask, snorkel and flippers as well as energy bars and binoculars in your daypack and head out the door.

Once you hit the sand, you sit down and open the guidebook you bought before coming on vacation. Which way should you go first? You're still a little tired from the early morning flight, but you're also keen to get exploring.

As you study the map, you hear a couple of kids coming towards you down the beach.

"Hi, I'm Adam," a blond haired boy says as he draws near.

"And I'm Jane."

The boy and girl are about your age and dressed in swimming shorts and brightly colored t-shirts, red for him and yellow for her. They look like twins. The only difference is that the girl's hair is tied in a long ponytail while the boy's hair is cropped short. Both are brown and have peeling noses. By their suntans you suspect they've been at the resort a few days already.

"What are you reading?" Adam asks.

"It's a guide book. It tells all about the wildlife and the volcano. It also says there might be pirate treasure hidden here somewhere. I'm just trying to figure out where to look first."

Jane clasps her hands in front of her chest and does a tiny hop. "Pirate treasure, really?"

Adam looks more skeptical, his brow creases as he squints down at you. "You sure they just don't say that to get the tourists to come here?"

"No, I've read up on it. They reckon a pirate ship named the *Port-au-Prince* went down around here in the early 1800s. I thought I might go exploring and see what I can find."

"Oh can we help?" Jane says. "There aren't many kids our age staying at the moment and lying by the pool all day gets a bit boring."

"Yeah," Adam agrees. "I'm sure we could be of some help if you tell us what to do. I have a video camera on my new phone. I could do some filming."

There is safety in numbers when exploring, and three sets of eyes are better than one. But if you do find treasure, do you want to share it with two other people?

It is time to make your first decision. Do you:

Agree to take Adam and Jane along?

Or

Say no and go hunting for treasure on your own?

114

Preview: The Sorcerer's Maze

Your feet are sinking into a marshmallow floor. You take a few quick steps and find you can stay on top if you keep moving. How did you get here? One moment you were reading and now you're in a long hallway. The place smells of candy and the pink walls are soft when you poke them.

There is a sign hanging from the ceiling that says: YOU ARE AT THE BEGINNING OF THE SORCERER'S MAZE. But how do you get through to the end of the maze?

Down at the end of the hallway is an old red door. Maybe you should start there?

You take a few bouncy steps, your arms held out to help keep your balance. Getting up would be hard. You don't want to fall.

At last, you make it to the red door and try the doorknob. It's locked. You pace in a circle to stop from sinking. When you turn back to the door, you find another sign. On this sign is a question. Below the question are two possible answers. Maybe answering the question correctly will let you open the door.

The questions reads: What is the largest planet in our solar system?

It's time to make your first decision. You may pick right, you may pick wrong, but still the story will go on. What shall it be? Is it:

Jupiter? Or Saturn?

Preview: Dragons Realm

"Hey, Fart-face!"

Uh oh. The Thompson twins are lounging against a fence as you leave the corner store – Bart, Becks, and Bax. They're actually the Thomson triplets, but they're not so good at counting, so they call themselves twins. Nobody has dared tell them different.

They stare at you. Bart, big as an ox. Becks, smaller but meaner. And Bax, the muscle. As if they need it.

Bart grins like an actor in a toothpaste commercial. "What have you got?" He swaggers towards you.

Becks sneers, stepping out with Bax close behind. "Come on, squirt, hand it over," she calls, her meaty hands bunching into fists.

Your backpack is heavy with goodies. Ten chocolate bars and two cans of tuna fish for five bucks – how could you resist? And now you could lose it all.

The twins form a human wall, blocking the sidewalk. There's no way around them.

Seriously? All this fuss over chocolate? Not again! They've been bullying you and your friends for way too long. There's still time to outsmart them before the bus leaves for the school picnic.

A girl walks between you and the twins. You make your move, sprinting off towards the park next to school. Your backpack is heavy, but you've gained a head start on those numb skulls.

Becks roars.

"Charge," yells Bax,

"Get the snot-head," Bart bellows. Their feet pound behind you as you make it around the corner through the park gate. Now to find a hiding place.

On your right is a thick grove of trees. They'll never find you in there, not without missing the bus to the picnic.

To your left, is a sports field. Behind the bleachers, there's a hole in the fence. If you can make it through that hole, you're safe. They're much too big to follow.

Their pounding footsteps are getting closer. They'll be around the corner soon.

It is time to make a decision. Do you:

Race across the park to the hole in the fence?

Or

Hide from the Thompson twins in the trees?

Preview: Pirate Island

Your family is on holiday at a lush tropical island resort in the Caribbean. But you're not in the mood to sit around the pool with the others, you want to go exploring. Rumors say that pirate treasure has been found in these parts and you're keen to find some too. With a few supplies in your daypack, you fill your drinking bottle with water, grab your mask and snorkel, and head towards the beach.

You like swimming, but you've been planning this treasure hunt for months and now is as good a time as any to start. The beach outside the resort stretches off in both directions. To your right, it runs past the local village, where children laugh as they splash and play in the water. Palm trees line the shore and brightly colored fishing boats rest on the sand above the high tide mark. Past the village, way off in the distance is a lighthouse.

To your left, the sandy beach narrows quickly and soon becomes a series of rocky outcrops jutting into the sea. Steep cliffs rise up from the rocky shore to meet the stone walls of an old and crumbling fortress.

You have four hours before your family expects you back. It is time to make your first decision. Do you:

Go right and head towards the lighthouse?

Or:

Go left and head towards the rocks and the old fortress?

Preview: Deadline Delivery

Out of breath from climbing stairs, you finally reach Level 8 of Ivory Tower. Down the hallway, past a tattoo parlor, Deadline Delivery's neon sign glows red. The word Dead flickers as you approach.

It's two minutes past seven in the morning – is Deadline Delivery's dispatch office open yet? Yes, through the mesh-covered window in the steel door, Miss Betty is slouched behind her cluttered desk. You knock and smile as if you want to be here.

Miss Betty turns and scowls at you. Nothing personal – she scowls at everyone. She presses a button and the steel door squeaks and squeals open.

"Good morning, ma'am. Got any work for me today?" you ask.

She sighs, scratches her left armpit, and taps at her computer. Then she rummages through a long shelf of packages and hands you a plastic-wrapped box and two grimy dollar coins. "Urgent delivery," she says. "Pays ten bucks, plus toll fees."

Ten dollars is more than usual. Suspicious, you check the box's delivery label. "390 Brine Street? That's in the middle of pirate territory!"

She shrugs. "If you're too scared, there are plenty of other kids who'll do it."

Scared? You're terrified. But you both know she's right – if you don't take this job, someone else will. And you really need the money – you have exactly three dollars in the whole world, and your last meal was lunch yesterday. "Thank you, Miss Betty."

"Uniform," she says, pointing to the box of Deadline Delivery caps.

You pick up the least dirty cap. What's that stink? Has something died in it? You swap it for the second-least dirty one and put that on. You'd rather not wear any kind of uniform – sometimes it's better to not attract attention in public – but Miss Betty insists.

The steel door squeaks and starts to close, and you hurry out. Miss Betty doesn't say goodbye. She never does.

After stashing the package in your backpack and the toll coins in your pocket, you hurry down the stairs to the food court on Level 5. Time to grab a quick breakfast. This might be your last meal ever, and there's no sense in dying hungry. This early in the morning, only Deep-Fried Stuff and Mac's Greasy Spoon are open, so there's not a lot of choice.

In Mac's Greasy Spoon, Mac himself cuts you a nice thick slice of meatloaf for a dollar, and you smile and thank him, even though his meatloaf is always terrible. If there's any meat in it, you don't want to know what kind. At least it's cheap and filling. After a few bites, you wrap the rest in a plastic bag and put it in your pocket for lunch.

You walk back down the stairs to Ivory Tower's main entrance on Level 3. Levels 1 and 2 are somewhere further down, underwater, but you've never seen them. The polar ice caps melted and flooded the city before you were born.

From beside the bulletproof glass doors, a bored-looking guard looks up. "It's been quiet out there so far this morning," she tells you, as she checks a security camera screen. "But there was pirate trouble a few blocks north of the Wall last night. And those wild dogs are roaming around again too. Be careful, kid."

The doors grind open, just a crack, enough for you to squeeze through and out onto Nori Road. Well, everyone calls it a road, although the actual road surface is twenty feet under the murky water. Both sides of the so-called road have sidewalks of rusty girders and planks and bricks and other junk, bolted or welded or nailed to the buildings – none of it's too safe to walk on, but you know your way around.

Just below the worn steel plate at your feet, the water's calm. Everything looks quiet. No boats in sight. A few people are fishing out their windows. Fish for breakfast? Probably better than meatloaf.

Far over your head, a mag-lev train hums past on a rail bridge. Brine Street's only a few minutes away by train – for rich people living up in the over-city. Not you. Mac once told you that most over-city people never leave the sunny upper levels, and some of them don't even don't know the city's streets are flooded down here. Or don't care, anyway. Maybe that's why there are so many security fences between up there and down here, so that over-city people can pretend that under-city people like you don't exist.

There are fences down here too. To your left, in the distance, is Big Pig's Wall – a heavy steel mesh fence, decorated with spikes and barbed wire and the occasional skeleton. The same Wall surrounds you in every direction, blocking access above and below the waterline – and Brine Street's on the other side. The extra-dangerous side.

Big Pig's Wall wasn't built to keep people in – no, it's to keep pirates out.

The heavily guarded Tollgates are the only way in or out, and to go through them, everyone has to pay a toll to Big Pig's guards. A dollar per person, more for boats, all paid into big steel-bound boxes marked Donations. Big Pig has grown rich on those "donations". Not as rich as over-city people, but still richer than anyone else in this neighborhood. Some people grumble that Big Pig and his guards are really no better than the pirate gangs, but most locals think the tolls are a small price to pay for some peace and security.

Then again, you happen to know the Tollgates *aren't* the only way in and out – last week, you found a secret tunnel that leads through the Wall. No toll fees if you go that way – two dollars saved. You finger the coins in your pocket.

It's time to make a decision. How will you get to Brine Street? Do you:

Go the longer and safer route through a Tollgate?

Or

Save time and money, and try the secret tunnel?

Preview: Dinosaur Canyon

A meteorite streaks across a cloudless Montana sky and disappears behind a hill, not far away.

"Anyone see that?" you say to your classmates as you point towards the horizon.

Around the bus, a couple of students look up from their phones. "What? Huh?"

"The meteorite. Did you see it?"

"Meteor what?" the kid sitting next to you asks.

"Never mind." You shake your head and wonder if you're the only one who's really interested in this fieldtrip.

"I saw it," Paulie Smith says from a seat near the back. "That was amazing!"

As you and Paulie search the sky for more meteorites, the bus turns off the main road and passes an old wooden sign. WELCOME TO GABRIEL'S GULCH.

"Right," Mister Jackson says, as the bus comes to a stop. "Once your tents are set up, you've got the afternoon to go exploring. So get to it. And remember, take notes on what you see and hear. You *will* be tested."

You're hoping to find some fossils. You might even get lucky and stumble across a piece of that meteorite. That would be awesome.

After locating a level patch of ground near a clump of saltbush, you set up your dome tent and toss your sleeping bag and air mattress inside with the rest of your gear. Then you grab your daypack and water bottle. You'd never think of going for a hike without taking water with you. They don't call this area the *Badlands* without good reason.

A couple of energy bars, an apple, compass, box of matches, waterproof flashlight, folding army shovel and some warm clothing go into your daypack as well, just in case.

Mister Jackson is drinking coffee with some parents who've come along to help. They've set up the kitchen near the junction of a couple of old stone walls as protection from the wind and are laughing and telling tales of other camping trips.

"My tent's up Mister J, so I'm off to look around."

He nods. "Make sure you fill in the logbook with your intentions. Oh, and who're you teaming up with? Remember our talk on safety – you're not allowed to go wandering about alone. And watch out for rattlesnakes."

You look at the chaos around camp. Rather than being interested in dinosaur fossils, which is the main reason for this trip, most of your fellow students are puzzling over how their borrowed tents work or complaining about the cell phone reception. Camping equipment is strewn everywhere. Apart from you, Paulie is the only one who's managed to get his tent up so far.

"Hey, Paulie. I'm heading out. Want to tag along?"

Paulie points to his chest. "Who? Me?"

Paulie's not really a friend. He's a year behind you at school, but at least he seems interested in being here. He's even got a flag with a picture of a T. Rex working at the front counter of a burger joint, flying over his tent. Chuckling, you ponder the silliness of a short-armed dinosaur flipping burgers

"Yeah, you, get a move on." You walk over and write in the camp's logbook. *Going west towards hills with Paulie. Back in time for dinner.*

"What are we going to do?" Paulie asks.

"Explore those hills," you say, pointing off into the west. "Quick, grab your pack and let's go … before Mr. J or one of the parents decide to come along."

As Paulie shoves a few supplies in his bag, you look across the scrubland towards the badly eroded hills in the distance. It's ideal country for finding fossils. Erosion is the fossil hunter's best friend. Who knows what the recent rains have uncovered for a sharp-eyed collector like yourself.

"Did you know they've found Tyrannosaurus Rex bones around here?" Paulie says as the two of you head out of camp.

You pull the *Pocket Guide to the Montana Badlands* out of your back pocket and hold it up. "I've been reading up too."

"But did you know scientists reckon T. Rex had arms about the same length as man's but would have been strong enough to bench press over 400 pounds?"

"Yeah?" you say, remembering Paulie's love of obscure facts and how he drives everyone at school crazy with them. "Well according to this book, there's been more dinosaur fossils found in Montana than anywhere else in the country."

Paulie nods. "I want to find an Ankylosaurus. They're built like a tank with armor and everything. They had horns sticking out of the sides of their heads and a mean looking club on the end of their tails!"

That would be pretty awesome. "A tank eh? Maybe we'll find one of its scales embedded in the rock, or a horn sticking out of a cliff. Anything's possible when fossil hunting, that's what makes it so exciting."

You both stride off across the prairie with big smiles and high hopes. Fifteen minutes later, when you look back, the camp is nothing but a cluster of dots barely visible through the sagebrush.

"Where to from here?" Paulie asks.

"There's a couple of options. We could search for that meteorite. It must have come down somewhere around here."

"Maybe it landed in that canyon?" Paulie says, indicating a gap between two hills. "Could be all sorts of neat stuff in there."

"That's Gabriel's Gulch," you say, referring to the map in your guide. "Or we could look for fossils in those hills," you say, pointing to your right. "According to the guide, there's an abandoned mine over there too."

Your adventure is about to begin. It is time to make your first decision. Do you:

Go left into Gabriel's Gulch?

Or

Go right towards the eroded hills?

You Say Which Way Adventures

Between The Stars
Pirate Island
Lost in Lion Country
Once Upon An Island
Deadline Delivery
Secrets of Glass Mountain
Danger on Dolphin Island
Volcano of Fire
The Sorcerer's Maze Adventure Quiz
The Sorcerer's Maze Jungle Trek
The Creepy House
Dragons Realm
Dinosaur Canyon

YouSayWhichWay.com